"About that kiss on the dance floor," he began.

"I don't want to talk about that kiss."

"We need to talk about the kiss." He reached out and captured her hand in his.

"It shouldn't have happened," she said, trying, and failing, to pull away from him. "It was a momentary lapse of judgment."

"I think it was the natural reaction of a man and a woman who are attracted to each other."

"We are work partners."

"We're human beings, not robots." He rubbed his thumb across her knuckles, sending a current of sensation through her, like an electrical charge.

She jerked her hand away from him. "We have a job to do," she said. "We can't make this about us."

RUNNING OUT OF TIME

CINDI MYERS

Special thanks and acknowledgment are given to Cindi Myers for
her contribution to the Tactical Crime Division miniseries.

Recycling programs
for this product may
not exist in your area.

ISBN-13: 978-1-335-13586-5

Running Out of Time

Copyright © 2020 by Harlequin Books S.A.

Harlequin Enterprises ULC
22 Adelaide St. West, 40th Floor
Toronto, Ontario M5H 4E3, Canada
www.Harlequin.com

Printed in U.S.A.

Cindi Myers is the author of more than fifty novels. When she's not crafting new romance plots, she enjoys skiing, gardening, cooking, crafting and daydreaming. A lover of small-town life, she lives with her husband and two spoiled dogs in the Colorado mountains.

Books by Cindi Myers

Harlequin Intrigue

Running Out of Time

Eagle Mountain Murder Mystery: Winter Storm Wedding

Ice Cold Killer
Snowbound Suspicion
Cold Conspiracy
Snowblind Justice

Eagle Mountain Murder Mystery

Saved by the Sheriff
Avalanche of Trouble
Deputy Defender
Danger on Dakota Ridge

The Ranger Brigade: Family Secrets

Murder in Black Canyon
Undercover Husband
Manhunt on Mystic Mesa
Soldier's Promise
Missing in Blue Mesa
Stranded with the Suspect

The Men of Search Team Seven

Colorado Crime Scene
Lawman on the Hunt
Christmas Kidnapping
PhD Protector

Visit the Author Profile page at Harlequin.com.

CAST OF CHARACTERS

Special Agent Laura "Smitty" Smith—A disciplined agent who never breaks the rules, Laura must go undercover as a newlywed to find the person responsible for a rash of poisonings and bombings in a small West Virginia town.

Special Agent Jace Cantrell—The military veteran and special ops expert has a reputation as a rebel and a rule breaker—exactly the kind of man to clash with Laura, yet the two must pose as husband and wife to solve a case that brings death to their very doorstep.

Donna Stroud—The head of Stroud Pharmaceuticals intends to keep her company going and her family together in the face of tragedy, but how far will she go to do so?

Parker Stroud—Donna's son chafes at his parents' unwillingness to put him in charge of the family business.

Merry Winger—Parker's girlfriend has big plans to marry Parker, despite his parents' disapproval of their relationship and Parker's own reluctance to make their relationship public.

Leo Elgin—His mother was poisoned by tainted medication manufactured by Stroud. He holds a grudge against the Stroud family.

Tactical Crime Division—Rapid-deployment joint team of FBI agents specializing in hostage negotiation, missing persons, IT, profiling, shootings and terrorism with director Jill Pembrook at the head.

Prologue

Who knew death could be so satisfying?

Half the people in town had gathered, watching police—every cop in the county from the looks of it—mill about while the paramedics wheeled out the gurney, the body on it covered by a sheet. Whispering, like the rush of wind through catalpa trees, rose from the crowd as people speculated on the identity of the person under the sheet. Mayville, West Virginia, population 2,000, was small enough that almost everyone knew everyone else.

But they didn't know each other. Not really. They didn't know what people were really capable of doing.

This was the third death in as many days. No one felt safe anymore. Things they had taken for granted—something they had trusted—had turned deadly. Eat too much chili at lunch? Pop a Stroud's Stomach Soother. Stress have your guts in a knot? Stroud's Stomach Soothers to the rescue. Safe and Natural—Our Promise to You. It said so right on the label.

Not so safe now.

A woman broke into sobs. Tammy somebody, who worked on the factory floor. "How can this be happening?" she wailed. "This used to be such a safe place."

Two other women moved in to comfort Tammy. The men around them shuffled their feet and stared at the ground, their expressions grim. Fear hung in the air like diesel exhaust, a choking poison that threatened to kill the town.

The killer had done that. One person had brought a town—a whole region, even—to its knees.

What a rush to have that kind of power. Seeing the body on the gurney sparked an idea. The perfect way to solve problems.

Chapter One

"We've got another tough case on our hands." Jill Pembroke, director of the FBI's tactical crime division, surveyed her team from the head of the conference table in the Bureau's Knoxville headquarters. "One that requires a great deal of discretion."

Something in the director's tone made Agent Laura Smith sharpen her focus. Pembroke, with her well-cut silver hair and feminine suit, might be mistaken for a high society grandmother, but she was as hard-nosed as they came, and not prone to exaggeration. That she reminded her team of the need for discretion pointed to something out of the ordinary.

The door to the conference room opened and a man slipped in. Tall and rangy, Agent Jace Cantrell moved with the grace of an athlete. He nodded to the director and eased into the empty seat next to Laura. No apology for being late. Typical. Laura slid her chair over a couple of inches. Cantrell was one of those men who always seemed to take up more than his share of the available space.

"We're going to be investigating product tampering at Stroud Pharmaceuticals in Mayville, West Virginia." Director Pembroke stepped aside to reveal a slide showing a squat factory building set well back on landscaped grounds.

"The antacid poisonings." Agent Ana Ramirez spoke from her seat directly across from Laura. She tucked a strand of dark hair into the twist at the nape of her neck, polished nails glinting in the overhead light. "That story has been all over the news."

"Do the locals not want the FBI horning in?" Agent Davis Rogers—the only member of the team not wearing the regulation suit—sat back in his chair beside Ramirez, looking every bit the army ranger he had once been. "Is that why the extra discretion?"

"No, the local police are happy to turn this over to us," Pembroke said. She advanced to the next slide, a listing of the deaths—six so far, with two additional people hospitalized—attributed to Stroud's Stomach Soothers, a natural, organic remedy that claimed a significant share of the market as an alternative to traditional antacids. "This hasn't been released to the public, but the poison in the contaminated tablets was ricin."

Laura would have sworn the temperature in the air-conditioned room dropped five degrees.

"Any suggestion of a link to terrorism?" Hostage negotiator Evan Duran, bearded and brooding, spoke from the end of the table. "Anybody claiming credit for the deaths?"

Pembroke shook her head. "At this point, we aren't assuming anything. Obviously, we want to avoid panicking the public."

"The public is already panicked," Rowan Cooper, the team's local liaison, said. "People have been organizing boycotts of all Stroud products." She absently twisted a lock of her jet-black hair, brow furrowed. "We'll need a strategy for managing the public's response."

"The facility where the Stomach Soothers were manufactured has been closed for the time being and the product is being pulled from store shelves," Pembroke said. "But another facility in town, which manufactures other items, remains open, and the company has reduced hours and reassigned as many employees as possible to the single plant. The company, the town, even the state officials, are very anxious to downplay this tragedy and get Stroud up and running full-speed as soon as possible."

"Why do that?" Kane Bradshaw, Agent-at-Large, said. Laura hadn't noticed him until now, seated as he was behind her and apart from the rest, almost in the shadows. Kane always looked as if he'd just rushed in from an overnight surveillance, all wind-blown hair and shadowed eyes.

The fact that he was here spoke to the gravity of this case. While always on hand when the team needed him, he wasn't much on office decorum.

"Jobs." Cantrell's voice, deep and a little rough, like a man who smoked two packs a day, sent a shiver through Laura. He didn't smoke, but maybe he once had. "Stroud Pharmaceuticals is one of the biggest employers in Boone County," he continued. "The coal mines are shutting down, and there isn't a lot of other industry. Stroud has been a savior to the community. They—and the officials they elected—are going to do everything in their power to keep the company running and redeem its reputation."

"Even covering up murder?" Laura asked.

Cantrell turned to her, his gaze cool. "I doubt they want to cover it up, but they'll definitely downplay it and keep it quiet."

"They want us to help, but they don't want us to be obvious." The youngest member of the team, computer specialist Hendrick Maynard, jiggled his knee as he spoke. A genius who looked younger than his twenty-six years, Maynard never sat still.

"Precisely." Director Pembroke advanced to another slide of a small town—tree-shaded streets lined with modest homes, some worse for wear. A water tower in the distance displayed the word *Mayville* in faded green paint. "Agents Smith and Cantrell, you are to pose as a married couple and take jobs at the Stroud factory. Investigations so far point to the poisonings having originated from within the plant itself, so your job is to identify possible suspects and investigate. Agent Rogers, you'll be in town as well..."

Laura didn't hear the rest of the director's assignments. She was focused on trying to breathe and holding back her cry of protest. She and Cantrell? As a couple? The idea was ridiculous. He was rough, undisciplined, arrogant, scornful...

"You look like you just ate a bug." Cantrell leaned toward her, bringing with him the disconcerting aroma of cinnamon. His gravelly voice abraded her nerves. "Don't think I'm any more excited about this than you are."

"Do you have a comment, Agent Cantrell?" Pembroke asked.

He straightened. "I think Agent Smith is going to stick out like a sore thumb in Mayville. Everything about her screams blue blood as well as law enforcement."

"I've worked undercover before." Laura bristled. She didn't care what Cantrell thought of her, but to imply she wasn't capable of doing her job—

"I'm sure Agent Smith will adapt," Pembroke said. "Smitty, you'll be working as assistant to the plant director, Parker Stroud, son of company owners Steve and Donna Stroud. This should give you access to personnel files, as well as financial records and other information you might find useful. Agent Cantrell, you'll be on the manufacturing floor."

Where he'd fit right in, Laura thought. Cantrell had the Southern drawl and casual attitude of the classic regular-guy down pat.

"Our profiler, Dr. Melinda Larsen, will assist with evaluating suspects," Pembroke continued. "She'll be available to travel to Mayville if necessary. Agent Maynard is on call for research and anything else you need. Agent Rogers and Agent Ramirez will be the FBI's official representatives in the area and will be on location as backup."

Davis Rogers cracked his knuckles. "Happy to help."

"Smitty, you and Cantrell will need to report immediately to the support center for your background documents and everything you'll need to start your assignment. You'll depart for Mayville tomorrow. Rogers and Ramirez will be a few hours ahead of you." She surveyed the team again, then nodded, as if satisfied with what she saw. "Any questions?"

There were none. The team knew how to launch a new op and hit the ground running. "Then get to work." Pembroke dismissed them.

Laura pushed back her chair and started to stand. "Agent Smith, a word, please," Pembroke said.

Self-conscious over being singled out, Laura

kept her eyes on the table as the others left. Cantrell stood and slid a stick of gum into his mouth, then leaned over her chair. "Later," he said, with a cinnamon-scented grin.

When she and the director were alone, Pembroke sat beside her. "I know you're not happy about this assignment," the director said.

"I never said—" Laura began.

"You didn't have to say it." Pembroke smiled. "Your dislike of Agent Cantrell is clear, but he's very good at his job, and he has a connection to this region that makes him ideal for this assignment."

"Is he from Mayville?" Laura asked.

"He's from a small town in Tennessee. A town very similar in many ways to Mayville. He has an insight into the culture of the area that could prove very useful. I'm counting on you to rein in some of his more unorthodox tendencies."

Great. She was on this job to babysit.

"I also think this assignment will be good for you," Pembroke said. "You're very dedicated and skilled. You pay attention to details. Those are the skills this assignment requires. But you'll also need to make friends among the locals and attune yourself to the overall atmosphere. I know you prefer to work alone, so this assignment will help you build your skills at relying on others for help and information."

"I work with this team every day," Laura protested.

Pembroke nodded. "You do, but you also can be a bit…aloof. I believe it's this tendency to hold yourself a bit apart that's behind Agent Cantrell's belief that you'll have trouble fitting in at the factory. I'm counting on you to prove him wrong."

Laura did her best to hide any response to this criticism, though the director's words stung. So what if she wasn't one to hang out with her fellow agents after work or discuss her private life with them? She preferred to keep her personal and business lives separate, but that didn't mean she was as cold as Pembroke made her sound. "I'll do my best," she said.

"You always do." Pembroke rose, signaling an end to the meeting.

Laura rose also and was gathering her coffee cup and notebook when the door opened and a slim young man entered. "Sorry to interrupt, Director," he said. "But there's a call for you. It's urgent."

Pembroke nodded and walked to the phone in the corner of the room. Laura moved toward the door. She had just opened it when the director called to her. "Smitty, wait."

Laura turned. As the director continued to listen to whoever was on the other end of the line, some of the color drained from her face. "Yes,"

Pembroke said. "We'll get right on it." She hung up the phone, her expression grave.

"What is it?" Laura asked. "What's wrong?"

"That was West Virginia State Police Office. They've just learned that at least a dozen bottles of potentially tainted Stomach Soothers are unaccounted for."

"You mean consumers didn't turn them in?"

Pembroke shook her head. "According to the company's records, these bottles were never sent to stores. They're missing from the factory. They might have been stolen."

"Or the person who planted the ricin in the product originally has stashed them, maybe waiting until things calm down to release them again," Laura said. Like a deadly bomb the killer could set off to wreak havoc whenever he wanted.

Chapter Two

Driving down Main Street in Mayville, West Virginia, on Sunday afternoon gave Jace an itchy feeling between his shoulder blades, as if someone had slapped a target back there and he was bracing for the first shot. He had never been here before, but he already knew what he'd find: a mix of aching beauty in blooming azaleas and stately homes side-by-side with the despair of lost glory and opportunities passed by. Closed storefronts, weedy lots, and idle men and women paired with groups of laughing children, flourishing gardens and rolling fields.

He'd grown up in a place like this. His family—his parents and sister—still lived there. Whenever he visited, he couldn't wait to leave, smothered by all the problems he couldn't fix.

"It's not like I thought it would be," Smitty said.

He glanced at her strapped into the passenger seat of the ten-year-old mustard-colored Chevy pickup. Her blond hair, normally twisted back in a bun, hung loose around her shoulders, the no-name jeans and peasant top making her look younger and softer. More accessible.

He focused on the street once more. A man would be a fool to think there was anything soft or vulnerable about Agent Smith, especially where Jace was concerned. She didn't exactly curl her lip in disgust when he approached, but the expression was implied.

"What do you mean?" he asked, slowing the truck to allow an elderly couple—her with a walker, him with a cane—to cross the street.

"It's so quiet," she said. "It doesn't look like a place where violence has made national headlines. I expected more press, and people milling around."

He slid a fresh stick of cinnamon gum into his mouth from the pack that rested on the dash and then gave the truck some gas. "I imagine the powers that be are tamping down any hint of panic," he said. "From the media reports, the politicians are downplaying the poisonings as an attempted terrorist attack that has already been stopped."

"What about the dozen potentially poisoned bottles that are unaccounted for?"

"They haven't released that information to the press and they're counting on us to find them before anyone else dies."

She shuddered. "If someone else does die, the politicians will be pointing their fingers at us."

"If that bothers you, you should be in another line of work."

She stiffened, just as he had known she would. "I take a great deal of pride in the work the Bureau does," she said. "As should you."

"But I don't waste time worrying about what a bunch of pencil pushers and pontificators think of me," he said.

"Except those are the people who sign the bills that ultimately pay your salary," she said.

"They need people like me more than I need people like them." He glanced at her. "If you remember that, it makes the job a lot easier."

"Easier to cut corners and ignore the regulations, you mean."

He grinned. "That, too."

She made a noise in her throat almost like a growl. Kind of sexy, but if he told her that, she would rightly blow a gasket. Smitty was the poster child for "wound too tight."

"We need to figure out who has it in for the Strouds," he said.

"You think that's what's behind this?" she asked. "Destroy their reputation by sabotaging their most popular product?"

"Don't you?"

She didn't answer right away, staring out at the passing scenery—a park with a bronze statue of a coal miner in overalls and hard hat, lunch bucket in one hand, a pick over his shoulder. Jace's father could have been the model for that statue, before he got sick.

"Maybe the goal isn't to destroy the Strouds," Smitty said. "You said yourself the town depends on the company for jobs. Maybe someone has a grudge against Mayville. And there's always the possibility that the target was one of the people who died, and everyone else is just a way to muddy the waters."

"Maybe," he said. "Whoever it is isn't being subtle. Ricin isn't like putting a little rat poison in someone's soup and hoping you used enough to do the job. It only takes a few grains of ricin to kill."

"Maybe we'll know more after we visit the factory."

"Rogers is supposed to brief us later today, after he and Ramirez meet with the local cops. Meanwhile, we have to move in." The back of the truck held everything a down-on-their-luck young couple might deem worth transporting to a new home—clothes, kitchen items, a television, and an antique chest of drawers that was someone's idea of a family heirloom. The Bureau's support center was known for its attention to detail. They had also supplied identification for Jason and Laura Lovejoy—a surname Jace was certain was someone's idea of a joke. The rental they were moving into was supposed to be furnished with everything else they'd need.

He turned the truck onto an unpaved side street identified by a leaning green sign as Lover's Lane.

"You have got to be kidding me." Smitty sneered at the sign.

"It's probably just the first suitable place they found to rent," Jace said. He watched the addresses on the mailboxes at the end of each drive and turned into the rutted lane at the very end of the street. The trailer was a rectangular white metal box with faded blue metal shutters, set well back from the road in the shade of a catalpa tree, the large heart-shaped leaves a brilliant green, the faded orchid-like blossoms littering the ground around the tree.

"Not what I was expecting." Smitty ground out the words through clenched teeth.

"It fits the profile," Jace said, shutting off the truck's engine. "We're broke newlyweds, remember? Besides, it's at the end of the road, with no close neighbors to spy on us."

Smitty got out of the truck, and he followed her up a two-foot-wide crushed gravel path to a porch, apparently made of old pallets, at the front of the trailer. She climbed the steps, inserted the key in the lock and shoved open the door.

They stood frozen for a moment, taking in the dark wood paneling, avocado-green carpet, and faux-leather sofa and matching recliner, complete with duct tape patches. The room smelled faintly of stale cigarette smoke. Smitty made a strangled sound, took a step forward and did a slow turn. "At least it looks clean." Her eyes met his. "I've never lived in a trailer before."

He had, but he wasn't going to share that with her. "Let's unload the truck," he said, and moved back outside.

She didn't immediately follow. He lowered the tailgate of the truck and pulled out a square cardboard box labeled KITCHEN. By the time he'd made it up the walkway with this burden, Smitty was waiting for him on the porch. "We have a problem," she said.

"What is it?" Jace moved past her and carried the box to the kitchen table, a metal and Formica relic from the 1960s. A hipster might have deemed it charmingly vintage, while his parents had discarded theirs years ago as a piece of junk.

"There's only one bed," Smitty said.

"The rental agreement said two bedrooms." The document, complete with their own expertly forged signatures, had been included with all their other paperwork.

"There are two bedrooms, but only one bed," she said. The faint worry lines on her high forehead deepened.

He shrugged. "So we'll get another bed tomorrow."

"What are we going to do tonight?"

"I guess you can either share the bed with me

or sleep on the couch." He gave her a wolfish grin—primarily because he knew it would get a rise out of her.

Sure enough, her cheeks turned rosy and sparks all but snapped from her blue eyes. "Why should you get the bed?" she demanded.

Because we're equal colleagues and any other time you'd be insulted at being treated with deference because you're a woman. "Because I'm bigger and taller. You fit the couch better. Of course, I'm always willing to share."

She twisted the plain gold band on the ring finger of her left hand. He wondered if she would take it off and throw it at him. "That is no way to speak to a fellow agent," she said.

"No. But it's how I might speak to my wife."

She was saved from having to think of a retort by the crunch of tires on gravel. They both turned to watch a silver Honda creep up the drive and stop behind the truck. Agent Davis Rogers unfolded his tall frame from the driver's seat and stood, hands on hips, studying the trailer. Sun burnished the dark brown skin of his bare arms and glinted on the steel frames of his Wayfarers.

Smitty moved ahead of Jace to greet Rogers at the door. "This looks like a cozy little love nest," Rogers said.

"Where are you staying?" Smitty asked.

He tucked the sunglasses into the neck of his

pale blue polo shirt. "The Magnolia Inn on the other side of town."

Jace was pretty sure the Magnolia Inn was a few stars down from wherever Smitty was used to staying, but he'd have bet she would have traded places with Rogers in a heartbeat.

"I'll help you unload the rest of your stuff and we'll talk," Rogers said.

It didn't take long for the three of them to move the assorted boxes and bags into the trailer. While Smitty opened windows, Jace made coffee, then they gathered around the kitchen table. "Ramirez and I met with the local police department," Rogers said. "They seem pretty competent and did a good initial investigation, given their limited resources. As we already know, they think the Stomach Soother poisoning was done prior to the safety seals being applied. There was no sign of tampering with the packaging in the bottles they've been able to recover."

One of Jace's goals working on the factory floor was to determine who might have tampered with the product, and how. "What about the missing bottles?" he asked.

"Stroud's computer system assigns a bar code to every bottle at the plant," Rogers said. "Those bar codes are matched to shipments that go to each store. If someone uses a store loyalty card when they make a purchase, they can even tie a specific bottle to a specific customer. They were able to recall most of the suspect medication that way. These twelve bottles, however, never went to a store or made it to a consumer. They disappeared shortly after they were filled."

"What do you mean, disappeared?" Smitty asked.

"They show up on the records as having been manufactured," Rogers said. "There's no trace of them after that."

"Does that happen often?" she asked. "Maybe employees help themselves?"

"The potential has to be there," Jace said. "But with these jobs, if you're even suspected of stealing, you're out on the street. And I'll bet they have cameras on the factory floor."

Rogers nodded. "The local cops say if the Strouds have ever had trouble with employees lifting product, they've handled it themselves."

"What do the Strouds say?" Smitty asked.

"Ramirez is talking to Donna Stroud right now. She's also making sure everything is set for you two to show up tomorrow as the newest employees of Stroud Pharmaceuticals." He grinned. "Better you than me."

BALLOONS, FLOWERS AND a couple of stuffed animals decorated a section of chain link fence in front of the headquarters of Stroud Pharmaceuticals. A stiff breeze rattled the ends of a ribbon bow tied to a vase of wilting daisies as Agent

Ana Sofia Ramirez walked past. She stopped to study the display. The flowers lay in front of a hand-lettered sign on white poster board. "We'll never forget you, Gini," it read.

Virginia Elgin, chief financial officer of Stroud Pharmaceuticals, had been the third person to die after using the contaminated Stomach Soothers. The bottle, found in her desk, had been traced to a local grocery store, as had the bottles that contained the tablets that had killed Herbert Baker and Gail Benito, the first two victims. The other five victims, three of whom had died, had purchased their Stomach Soothers from two different stores in a county directly east of Mayville.

Would the missing bottles turn up on yet another store's shelves, or in the medicine cabinet of the next victim? Were they merely lost in the system, or stashed on a shelf in the killer's closet, waiting to stir up a new panic?

Donna Stroud was a middle-aged woman with dyed black hair in a sensible cut, dressed for business even on a Sunday afternoon in flat shoes and the type of pantsuit that had never been in or out of fashion. She greeted Ana with a firm handshake. "Thank you for coming, Agent Ramirez. My husband and I are anxious to do anything we can to get to the bottom of this tragedy. I appreciate you meeting with me on a Sunday. I hate to upset the staff any more than I have to."

"We appreciate your cooperation," Ana said.

"I've reviewed all the information you gave local and state law enforcement," she continued when she was seated in front of Donna's desk, a scarred oak model whose surface was obscured by towers of precariously leaning paperwork. "When did you discover that some of the product in the batch in question was unaccounted for?"

"My son brought it to my attention yesterday afternoon. I notified the state police right away."

"That would be Parker Stroud, the plant manager?"

"Yes. He was in charge of verifying the inventory reports and noticed the discrepancy. Everyone is putting in overtime, trying to determine how this could have happened."

"Has anything like this ever happened before—inventory going missing?"

"No!"

Ana didn't hide her skepticism. "You've never had an employee decide to, say, help herself to a box of something?"

"No." Donna leaned across the desk toward Ana. "We have a zero-tolerance policy for that sort of thing. Employees and their belongings are subject to search at any time, and we have closed-circuit TV monitoring all parts of the factory. Beyond that, we're very careful about who we hire. We screen potential employees thoroughly, train them well, and I'm proud to say we have an industry-high retention rate. We have employees who have worked for Stroud for twenty years."

"So you don't have anyone you suspect might be responsible for contaminating the Stomach Soother tablets?"

"No one."

Donna Stroud looked Ana in the eye when she spoke. She was clearly weary, and frightened. But Ana didn't think she was lying. "We're hoping our agents here at the facility will be able to spot irregularities you may not have noticed," Ana said. "We appreciate your willingness to allow us access."

Donna sat back. "It's not as if I have much choice, is it? But I'd like to be allowed to inform Parker about what's going on. After all, one of the agents will be working under him, and the other will be right in his office."

"No." Ana spoke as firmly as she could. "It's imperative that as few people know about this operation as possible. If you'll remember, that was part of the agreement we reached that allows you to keep the rest of your facility still operating. If you don't feel you can uphold that agreement…" She let the words hang, an implied threat.

The lines around Donna's mouth tightened. "I understand."

Ana stood. "The Lovejoys will be here for orientation at 8:00 a.m. tomorrow." She handed over a business card. "If you think of anything that

might be helpful to the investigation, or spot anything suspicious, don't hesitate to call me. That's
my direct number and I'll answer anytime, day
or night."

Donna stood also, weariness bowing her shoulders. "Thank you, Agent Ramirez," she said. "I
hope you can get to the bottom of this quickly.
Then we can at least begin to get back to normal."

She escorted Ana out of her office. They
passed a side door marked V. Elgin, CFO. Ana
stopped. Donna followed her gaze to the door.
"As horrible as all of this is, it's even more horrible, losing Gini," she said, her voice tight with
emotion.

"I understand she died here, at the office?"
Ana asked.

Donna nodded. "She came back from lunch
and was working in there, with the door closed.
One of the admins went in to discuss the agenda
for an upcoming meeting and found her." She
put a hand to her mouth. "We thought at first it
might have been a heart attack. She suffered from
chronic heartburn and we thought maybe it was
something more serious after all." She cleared
her throat. "When they told us it was the Stomach Soothers, we couldn't believe it."

"What do you know about ricin, Mrs. Stroud?"
Ana asked.

"They—well, the local police chief—told us
that was what was in the Stomach Soother tab-

lets. I know it's deadly… Maybe something terrorists have used elsewhere? Do you think this was done by terrorists?"

"We haven't reached any conclusions at this point. I won't take up any more of your time." She left the office, aware of Donna and several other women watching her walk away. She felt sorry for them, ordinary people caught in such a nightmare. But she wouldn't let her pity get in the way of doing her job. The most likely scenario involved someone inside the factory contaminating those tablets, which meant the Strouds and everyone who worked for them were potential suspects.

As she turned onto the sidewalk, she noticed a man standing in front of the makeshift memorial. He was young, early-to midtwenties, wearing new-looking jeans and a blue dress shirt unbuttoned and untucked over a gray T-shirt. She stopped and studied him. He looked out of place. Lost.

A trio of women, possibly factory workers on the weekend shift returning from a lunch break, approached. Ana caught their eye. "Who is that man?" she asked.

The oldest of the trio, an African American woman in her forties, glanced toward the memorial, and her expression changed to one of sorrow. "That's Miss Gini's boy, Leo."

"Gini Elgin?" Ana clarified.

A very pale woman with hair the color of carrots nodded. "He's real tore up about his mama's passing."

The third woman, brown-haired and freckled, made a face. "It's terrible about Miss Gini, but that Leo always was a little odd."

"What do you mean, odd?" Ana asked. Leo had moved closer to the memorial now, actually standing on some of the flowers, head bowed, hands shoved in the front pockets of his jeans.

"Just, odd," the woman said.

"Not friendly," the older woman said. "Real quiet. Now, Miss Gini was as friendly as could be, and not what you'd call quiet."

The others nodded. Then, as a group, they moved on. Ana continued down the sidewalk. When she was about ten feet from the memorial, Leo Elgin leaned down and snatched up the vase of flowers and hurled it over the fence. It smashed on the concrete on the other side, sending glass and petals flying. Then he turned and ran away, with the awkward gait of someone who doesn't run often. He didn't look at Ana as he passed, but she had a clear view of his face, his expression one of agony, tears streaming down his cheeks.

Chapter Three

Laura spent most of her first night in Mayville tossing and turning and deeply resenting Jace for sleeping so soundly. She could hear him snoring in the next room. After she finally managed to doze off she overslept, awoke in a panic and charged into the trailer's single bathroom to find a shirtless Cantrell, face half-covered in shaving cream, a straight razor in one hand.

Even half-asleep, she was impressed, both with the way he wielded the razor over his cheekbones and the impressive abs and pecs revealed in the anemic bathroom light. Stammering, she backed out of the room, his laughter trailing her all the way to the kitchen.

By the time he emerged from the bathroom, she was halfway through her first mug of coffee and had managed to rein in her racing heart. She ignored him and went to take her turn in the steamy shower, unsettled by the knowledge that he had been in here only moments before—naked. Then she was even more disturbed by the idea that he could hear her in here and might at this very moment be imagining *her* naked.

Clearly, she hadn't had nearly enough sleep. She and Cantrell were both professionals. She did not fantasize about her coworkers as a rule, so why should she assume he did? Then she remembered his wolfish grin when they had argued over the bed and bit back a groan.

When she returned to the kitchen, he shoved something wrapped in a paper towel in her hand. "We have to go now or we'll be late for our first day," he said.

"What is this?" She stared at the warm bundle in her hand.

"Fried egg sandwich."

"I don't eat fried foods." Her usual breakfast was a cup of yogurt or a piece of toast.

"Today you do." He handed her her purse. "Let's go. I'll drive and you can eat in the truck."

The sandwich was delicious, though she was aware of him watching her eat, which made her feel self-conscious and awkward. Then again, everything about this assignment was awkward.

The next hour passed in a blur. Laura suffered through an orientation that consisted of a ten-minute film about the history of Stroud Pharmaceuticals, a fifteen-minute drill on safety procedures and thirty minutes signing paperwork with her new fake name. Finally, she was directed to her new office, where she was greeted by a slender young man with thinning hair, oversized ears and a sour expression.

"Are you the new admin?" Parker Stroud, her new boss, asked.

"Yes, Laura Lovejoy." Laura offered her hand. He stared at it until she put it back down at her side.

"Great. Can you start by getting me some coffee?" He moved past her toward his office. "Two sugars," he called over his shoulder.

She retrieved the coffee from the machine in the adjacent break room and carried it in to him. Stroud was seated behind his desk, staring at a computer screen. He accepted the coffee and looked her up and down. "My mother said she hired you for this position," he announced. "What happened to Cheryl, the girl who was here before?"

The "girl" was fifty-five years old and had been temporarily relocated to work in the accounting department. "I'm not sure," Laura responded.

"No offense to you, but I'm thirty-four years old. I don't need my mother to pick out my secretary—excuse me, administrative assistant." He sipped the coffee, gaze lingering on her chest in a way that made her bristle. "Though I have to say, you're a lot better looking than Cheryl. And you know how to make a decent cup of coffee. So we'll see how it goes."

"Yes, sir." She tried to appear neutral in front of him, though inside, she seethed.

"Well, don't just stand there. Go back to your desk." He waved her away. "If I need you, I'll call you."

She returned to her desk and studied the row of old-fashioned filing cabinets along one wall. She'd investigate their contents under the pretense of organizing her workspace or something. Later, she'd attempt to hack into the firm's personnel and financial records. She could contact Maynard for help if she needed it.

She tucked a strand of hair behind her ear. She wasn't used to wearing it down at work, and it felt in the way. But the support office had deemed her usual chignon too sophisticated for the role she was playing.

She opened the top drawer of the first cabinet and stared at a row of files, each labeled with a month and a year. A quick flip through the first file revealed production records for the two manufacturing plants—one of which had produced all of the Stomach Soothers sold by Stroud's, the other responsible for herbal throat lozenges, a sleep aid and a preparation for teething infants.

"It's a little early in the day to be looking for an insomnia cure."

She hadn't heard the door to Parker's office open, and his voice right behind her startled her. She choked off a gasp, returned the file and shut the drawer, then turned to him with a smile firmly in place. "Did you need something, Mr. Stroud?"

"Call me Parker. Mr. Stroud is my father." He nodded toward the filing cabinets. "Every bit of this data is in our computer system, but my father insists on hard copy records. Just one of the many examples of how my parents are keeping this company from realizing its full potential."

"Surely you'll be in charge of the company one day," she said.

"Thinking you'll be moving up in the world if you stick with me?" he asked. "Don't hold your breath. My folks have made it clear they don't intend to let go of the reins for years to come. Though why they'd even want it now, I don't know."

"You mean, because of what happened with the Stomach Soothers?"

"Yeah, what else do you think I mean?"

She widened her eyes, feigning ignorance, hoping she wasn't overacting.

Apparently, Parker bought it. He rolled his eyes. "Go down to accounting and tell them I need last month's financials ASAP. And don't let them give you any nonsense about this whole business with the Stomach Soothers disrupting workflow. That isn't the only product we make and people have wallowed enough."

"Yes, sir." The way he said the words sounded

rehearsed, as if he'd been practicing a tough-guy act in front of a mirror. Maybe that was how he thought a hard-nosed CEO should behave.

She hurried out of the office, but slowed as soon as she turned the corner. Now was as good a time as any to familiarize herself with the layout of the building. She strolled the halls, opening and closing doors, locating the men's and women's restrooms, an empty classroom, a larger meeting room and the janitor's supply closet.

"Can I help you with something?" A round-faced young woman with a halo of brown curls, a sheaf of papers clutched to her chest, approached as Laura shut the door to the supply closet.

"I'm looking for the accounting department," Laura said.

"I'll show you." The woman motioned for Laura to follow, then set off down the hall, high heels clicking like castanets on the polished tile floor. "Ask for Angela," she said, indicating a frosted glass door, then turned and tap-tapped away.

Angela proved to be a middle-aged woman with flawless brown skin whose desktop was dominated by an oversized computer monitor. "Mr. Stroud needs the April financial reports," Laura said. "Parker Stroud," she clarified.

Angela frowned. "Today is the third. Those reports aren't compiled until the tenth. He knows that. And now you know it, so don't bother me again."

"Did he send me here to bother you to give me a hard time because I'm new, or does he do this every month?" Laura asked.

Angela's frown eased some. "Probably a little of both. Don't let him get to you. He's really okay, just a little tightly wound, I guess. A lot different from his mom and dad, that's for sure."

"I'd think everyone would be a little extra tense right now," Laura said.

"You got that right." She held out her hand. "Let's start over. My name is Angela Dupree. Welcome to Stroud Pharmaceuticals."

Laura took the hand, which was warm, smooth and beautifully manicured. "I'm Laura Lovejoy. I'm the new administrative assistant to Parker Stroud."

"This is a good place to work, despite the recent troubles," Angela said.

"Scary to think about the poisoning." Laura leaned toward Angela and lowered her voice. "I heard a reporter say the police think someone who worked at the plant must have put the poison in those bottles. Who would do such a horrible thing?"

"Nobody I know," Angela said. "And I think the reporters are wrong. I know it's a cliché to say a workplace is like a family, but we really are here at Stroud. No one has any reason to want to hurt people like that."

"That does make me feel a little better," Laura said. "Thanks."

"It was nice meeting you, but we both need to get back to work."

"Yes, ma'am."

Laura started to turn away, but Angela stopped her. "Laura?"

"Yes?"

"It would probably be a good idea if you didn't go around talking about the poisonings and such," she said. "People are pretty upset and it's not the best way to make a good impression."

"Gotcha. Thanks."

Laura wasn't worried about the kind of impression she made, except that getting people to like her might help her do her job. Had Angela warned her off because she was really trying to be helpful, or because she knew people here had things they wanted to hide?

"Who is that woman in with Angela?" Merry Winger craned her head around the edge of her computer screen to look toward the office. She had a view of a woman's slim back, long blond hair in graceful curls, slim-fit khaki trousers, low beige heels and a light blue shirt.

"That's Parker's new admin." Jerri Dunn followed Merry's gaze toward the office door. "She's a cutie, isn't she?"

"I didn't know they'd filled that position." Merry tried to hide her disappointment.

"Yeah, I think the job was only posted a week ago, but I guess they wanted to fill the spot quick."

Merry had put in for that position. It would have been ideal—she and Parker working together, seeing each other every day, not just a few times a month. He had an office with a locking door and a big desk—the fun they could have had in there. "You'd think they would choose someone from inside the company," she said.

"I gave up second-guessing decisions around here a long time ago," Jerri said.

Merry waited until the blonde left, then stood. "I'm going to the ladies'," she said.

She bypassed the ladies' room and headed for Parker's office. The blonde looked up from her desk when Merry entered. She was pretty enough, though kind of skinny and flat-chested. "Hello. May I help you?" she asked.

"I need to see Parker."

Merry started to walk past the desk, but the blonde stood. "Let me see if Mr. Stroud is available. What is your name?"

"Merry Winger. That's Merry, with two *r*'s and an *e*. Like *merry* Christmas." She wanted to make sure this woman knew exactly who she was. "And I'm sure Parker will want to see me."

"I'll let him know you're here." She knocked on Parker's door and, when he said "Enter," she slipped inside, leaving Merry to cool her heels in the outer office. He had better not refuse to see her. Not after all she'd done for him. Done with him.

The door opened and Parker followed the blonde out. "Merry, come in." He gestured toward the office. No smile of welcome, but then, Parker wasn't much for gestures of affection.

Parker shut the door behind them, but didn't move toward his desk. "What do you want?" he asked, keeping his voice low.

She pressed her palm against his chest and gave him a warm smile. "Maybe I just wanted to see you."

She stood on tiptoe and tried to kiss him, but he turned away. "I told you, not at work," he said.

She pouted. "Why not at work? Are you ashamed of me?"

"Of course not." He patted her shoulder. "But there are rules about executives dating workers. If anyone found out, we'd have to quit seeing each other and I don't want that, do you?"

If he married her, she wouldn't have to be an employee here anymore and that would solve the whole problem, but she knew better than to bring that up. Parker was the type of man who liked to think of things himself. "You're so considerate of me and my reputation," she said instead. "It's one of the things I love about you."

"Thanks for being so understanding. Now you'd better get back to work."

He urged her toward the door, but she resisted. She nodded toward the outer office. "Who is she?"

"The new girl?" He frowned. "I don't know. Someone my mom hired."

"You don't even get to pick out your own admin?"

"She's just a body behind a desk. I don't really care."

"I was hoping to get that job," she said. "Did you know I applied?"

"No, but it's just as well you didn't get it."

"Why not? Wouldn't you like having me around all the time?"

"I think it would be too distracting—for both of us." There was definite heat in his eyes now. A thrill shot through her. Whenever she started to worry he was getting tired of her, he always did something to quell her doubts. He really did care, he just had to be careful, given his position and all. She needed to be patient. When the time was right, they'd be together forever.

She left the office, even smiling at the new admin as she passed her desk. The blonde might look down her nose at Merry now, but she'd be singing a different tune when Merry was Mrs. Parker Stroud. By then, Parker would be running the whole business. And Merry would be running Parker.

LAURA WAITED UNTIL Merry and Parker were in Parker's office, then she moved to the door and pressed her ear to the gap between the door and the frame. A few moments later, she moved away. So Parker was fooling around with one of the office staff. That didn't strike her as a motive for mass poisoning. But she filed the information away as one more facet of the picture she was assembling of the company and its inner workings.

Promptly at five o'clock, Parker Stroud exited his office. "Go home," he told Laura. "No hanging around hoping for overtime."

"Good evening to you, too," she said.

He frowned and moved on.

She was searching Parker's desk a few minutes later when Cantrell strolled in. Jace. She needed to get used to thinking of him as Jace, so she wouldn't slip and address him as Cantrell, blowing their cover. Dressed in gray coveralls with his name in red script on the pocket, he still carried himself with a swagger. He was chewing gum—not smacking, but the muscles of his jaw bunched in a way she found distracting. He leaned on the doorjamb and watched her rifle through the desk drawers and peer under the blotter. "Find any-thing interesting?" he asked.

"Nothing." She shut the last drawer and moved toward him. "What about you?"

"I'm getting a feel for how this place operates. I can tell you, things aren't as watertight as the Strouds think. I'll fill you in at home. Let's get out of here."

They crossed the parking lot in a crowd of other workers leaving for the day. Heat billowed out of the cab of the truck when she opened the door, and she slid in carefully to avoid burning the back of her legs. Jace climbed into the driv-er's seat. "I'm starved," he said as he cranked the engine. "What's for dinner?"

"Why are you asking me?"

"I made breakfast. And lunch. It's your turn to cook."

Lunch had been a ham-and-cheese sand-wich. With mayonnaise, which she hated. She had pulled out the cheese and eaten it with the apple and fig cookies, which had been surpris-ingly good. Her stomach grumbled at the mem-ory. "Let's get takeout."

"Then your choices are pizza or barbecue."

They opted for barbecue, which was moist, smoky, spicy and some of the best food she had ever eaten.

"Director Pembroke says you grew up in a

place like this," she said, wiping sauce from her fingers with a paper napkin.

"Yeah."

"What was that like?"

"What do you want me to say? It was okay, until it wasn't."

"I'm just asking. Trying to be friendly."

Some of the tension went out of his shoulders. "Sorry. I grew up in Hatcher, Tennessee, which is a whole lot like Mayville. My mom and dad and sister still live there. My dad has had some health problems, so transferring to the Knoxville office means I can be around to help out more."

"I'm sorry to hear about your dad." She set aside the wadded-up napkin. "What's wrong with him? If you don't mind my asking."

"He has mesothelioma. A lung disease coal miners get from inhaling asbestos underground." He spoke very matter-of-factly, but his eyes wouldn't meet hers, as if he was afraid of revealing too much emotion.

"That must be rough," she said.

He shrugged. "What about you? Where did you grow up?"

"All over. My dad was in the military."

"That explains a lot."

"What do you mean by that?"

"Your 'don't color outside the lines' attitude. No offense. The military just ingrains that in you. I know. I was in the army for six years."

"You saw action?"

"Too much action. Fallujah. Baghdad, Kamdesh. It's how I ended up with the Bureau. They were recruiting military types."

She never would have described him as a "military type." "Davis Rogers came out of the military," she said.

"Yeah. He and I have compared notes. How did you end up with the feds?"

"I have a degree in forensic accounting from George Washington University, so it seemed like a good fit."

"Of course."

He spoke as if he had her all figured out. "What does that mean?" she demanded.

"You're a number cruncher. The whole coloring in the lines thing again. Don't get your back up. It's a useful skill. It'll probably be a big help with this case."

She forced herself to relax. They were never going to be able to work together if she took offense at everything he said. "You think money is behind the poisonings?"

"I think money has a lot to do with everything. And Stroud Pharmaceuticals is a multimillion-dollar concern."

"You said things in the factory aren't as secure as the Strouds like to portray. What did you find out?"

"I'll want to verify this, but apparently, the fa-

cility where the Stomach Soothers were manufactured is identical to this one. The surveillance
cameras are focused on the production area, but
not the break rooms or hallways or restrooms. I
think it would have been possible for someone
working with their back to the camera to slip the
poison into a batch of the tablets before the bottles were sealed."

"What about the missing bottles of Stomach
Soothers?"

"I haven't figured that out yet, but it's early
days. Anything suspicious in the front offices?"

She shook her head. "Parker Stroud is apparently involved with one of the women who works
in the offices, Merry Winger."

"What's Stroud like?"

She made a face. "Full of himself. Disdainful.
Kind of a jerk, but as far as I can tell, competent.
I got the impression he resents that his parents
don't want to retire and turn the whole business
over to him, but he was very clear that he stands
to inherit one day, so I can't see a motive for him
to destroy the company's reputation by poisoning
their most popular product."

"We should dig into the personnel files, see if
anyone has a grudge, maybe because they were
passed over for a promotion or something."

She nodded and was about to ask him more
about how the factory was set up when an ear-
piercing siren shrieked. All over the restaurant,

chairs were shoved back and people stood. "Fire alarm," a man said as he hurried past.

Another man pressed his cell phone to his ear. "It's at the plant," he said.

"Stroud's?" Laura asked.

The man nodded, then broke into a jog toward the parking lot. Jace threw some money on the table, and he and Laura joined the others leaving the restaurant. As he started the truck, both their cell phones rang.

"It's not a fire," he said, phone pressed to his ear.

"No." Ana Ramirez had just informed Laura of the reason for the alarm. "Someone planted a bomb at Stroud Pharmaceuticals."

Chapter Four

Yellow crime-scene tape flapped in a hot wind that carried the acrid scents of burning plastic and ash. Ana stood with Rogers just outside the tape, surveying what had once been a side entrance to Stroud Pharmaceutical Headquarters. The steel door, now grotesquely twisted, lay on the buckled sidewalk in front of a scorched hole rimmed by jagged brick. The windows on either side of the door had shattered and buckled. The area swarmed with fire and law enforcement personnel while farther back, dozens of Stroud employees and townspeople crowded against police barriers.

Rowan Cooper, the team's liaison officer, stepped through the wreckage of the doorway. A tall, slender woman with long black hair, Rowan was skilled at soothing ruffled feathers and persuading even the most reluctant law enforcement officers to cooperate with the FBI. She spotted Ana and Rogers and started toward them, followed by a stocky man with a gray buzz cut and heavy jowls. "This is Special Agent Terry Armand, ATF," Rowan said. "Terry, this is Special Agents Ana Sofia Ramirez and Davis Rogers."

They shook hands with the Alcohol, Tobacco, Firearms and Explosives agent. "What can you tell us about the explosion?" Rogers asked.

"Everything I can tell you is preliminary, but it looks like the explosive was wired to the door lock. Inserting a key in the lock set the trigger, and a few seconds later—enough time for someone to step inside—it went off. The bomb itself was a fairly simple pipe bomb. The damage is pretty typical." He glanced back toward the doorway.

"Would whoever planted that bomb need access to the interior of the area?" Rogers asked.

Armand nodded. "Oh yes. As best as we can determine at this preliminary stage, the bomb itself was located just inside the door."

"Whose key set off the explosion?" Ana asked.

"Lydia Green, forty-four," Rowan said. "She'd worked at Stroud for three years as an independent commercial cleaning service."

"I talked to a few people who said that door is kept locked and generally only used after hours," Armand said. "The plant is only running one shift right now, and that ended at five. Otherwise, many more people might have been injured."

"Was that intentional or coincidental?" Rogers

wondered. "We need to find out who had keys to that door."

"Here's the person who can tell us," Ana said.

They turned to watch Donna Stroud make her way through the crowd. She was still dressed in a boxy pantsuit and low heels. Only her red-rimmed eyes and pale face betrayed her distress. She hurried to join Ana, Rogers and the others on the sidewalk. "What is going on here?" she asked. "I thought you were here to help, and now this happens."

"Mrs. Stroud, have you or your husband or son received any threats?" Rogers asked. "Anyone trying to intimidate or coerce you?"

"If there was anything like that, I would have told you," she said. "We've been as cooperative as we know how to be." She looked back toward the ravaged doorway, her face a mask of pain. "Did the same person do this who poisoned the Stomach Soother tablets?"

"We don't know," Ana said. "Do you think there's a connection?"

"I don't know what to think." She shook her head. "They told me Lydia was killed. She has three children. What is going to happen to them now? What is going to happen to all of us?"

"Mrs. Stroud, where is your husband?" Ana asked. "Is he still out of town?"

The haunted look in her eyes increased. "My husband isn't well," she said.

Before Ana could ascertain the nature of his illness, a young man in jeans and a golf shirt elbowed his way through the crowd and jogged up to them. "I just heard the news," he said, putting his arm around the woman.

"My son, Parker Stroud," Donna said. "These are Agents Ramirez and Rogers, from the FBI." She frowned at Rowan and Terry. "I'm sorry, I don't know these people."

"It doesn't matter." Parker waved away the introductions and scowled at Rogers. "If you're the FBI, what are you doing to put a stop to this persecution of my family?"

"So you feel these attacks are personal?" Rogers asked. "Aimed directly at your family?"

"What else am I supposed to think?" Parker asked. "The Stroud family is Stroud Pharmaceuticals. This is clearly an attempt to destroy our reputation and our livelihood."

"Who has a key to that door?" Ana asked.

Donna took in a deep breath and moved out of her son's embrace. "I do, of course. Parker. Angela Dupree in accounting. Merry Winger, the accounting admin. Gini Elgin before she died. And of course, Lydia had a key so she could come in and clean." She pressed her lips tightly together.

"Was this Mrs. Green's usual time to enter the building to clean?" Ana asked.

"No." Donna paused and took a deep breath. "Most of the time, Lydia came in the morning, before the other employees reported for work. I like to get an early start myself, so I often saw her then. But this morning she reminded me that she was due to leave on vacation tomorrow, and would I mind if she cleaned tonight, so she could get an early start."

"How many people knew about this change of schedule?" Rogers asked.

"I'm not sure," Donna said. "I didn't mention it to anyone, but Lydia might have."

"What about Mr. Stroud?" Ana asked. "Does he have a key to that door?"

Donna exchanged a telling look with her son. "My father isn't well," he said.

"How exactly is he unwell?" Rogers asked.

"My husband suffers from early-onset dementia," Donna said.

"He's not able to participate fully in the business anymore," Parker said. "I do what I can to help my mother, though I could do more if she'd let me."

"I'm still capable of running this company," Donna said.

"What happened to Gini's key after she died?" Ana asked.

Donna's face clouded. "I don't know. I've been meaning to ask her son for it, but with so much else going on…" Her voice trailed away.

"Whoever set up that bomb knew only certain

people had the key to that entrance," Ana said. "It's possible one of those people was the target."

"That's too big a coincidence," Parker said. "This has to be related to the tampering with the Stomach Soothers."

"Then who do you think is targeting the company?" Ana asked. "Do you have a rival who would wish you harm? A disgruntled former employee? Or perhaps a personal enemy?"

"We don't have any of those things," Donna said. "This has to be random. Some kind of terrorist."

"Whoever did this, it's your job to find out and put a stop to it," Parker said.

"We fully intend to do so," Ana said. "And if you have any suspicions about anyone, be sure to share them with us."

"You might start by interviewing the Lovejoys. They just started work today and now this happens. That's a pretty odd coincidence, don't you think?"

Ana followed his gaze across the parking lot, to where Jace and Laura stood with a group of other employees. "I really don't think the Lovejoys had anything to do with this," Donna said.

"No, that's a good idea," Rogers said. "We'll be sure to talk to them. Is there anyone else you can think of who might be angry with you personally, or with the company in general?"

Donna stared at the ground but said nothing.

"There isn't anyone," Parker said.

"Gini Elgin's son was very upset when I spoke with him yesterday," Donna said. "He blames us for his mother's death. But he certainly didn't poison Gini. I think it was mostly grief talking. I remember him from when he and Parker went to school together, and he was always such a nice young man. Gini was very proud of him and I know her death has devastated him."

"What is his name?" Rogers took out his phone to make a note.

"Leo Elgin," Parker said. "But he didn't have anything to do with this. You're wasting your time with him."

"Have you spoken to him since he came back to town?" Donna asked her son.

"I haven't had time," Parker said. "I've been too busy trying to keep this company going."

"I think it would mean a lot to him if you touched base," Donna said.

Parker shook his head but made no reply.

"Is there a location near here we can use to interview people?" Ana asked.

"Can't you do that at the police station?" Parker asked.

"It would be easier if we had someplace closer." Ana said. "Since we'll need to talk to all your employees. It's possible one of them saw or heard something unusual."

"There's a conference room at the back of the

production plant across the parking lot," Donna said. "We use it sometimes for training. If there's anything else you need, let us know."

"Thank you," Rogers said. "We'll start with the Lovejoys. Agent Cooper, would you bring them to us, please?"

Rowan left to fetch Cantrell and Smitty. Donna turned away. Instead of following her, Parker moved closer to Ana. "If you learn anything, come to me first," he said. "My mother doesn't need any more stress right now. My father is a lot worse off than she wants to admit. That, along with everything else that has happened with the business, has her at her breaking point. I've been trying to persuade her to turn everything over to me, but she just can't give up that control."

"We'll share information with you as we are able," Ana said. But Donna Stroud was still president of Stroud Pharmaceuticals, and would be informed as well.

LAURA AND JACE kept up the pretense of not knowing Rogers, Ramirez and Rowan Cooper until they were all in the back conference room, which, as a precaution, the ATF had swept with bomb-sniffing dogs, and Rogers had checked for listening devices. Jace dropped into the chair across from Ramirez. "Before you ask, we haven't found out anything so far."

"Parker Stroud thinks you two are suspicious," Ramirez said.

"Both of us?" Laura glanced at Jace. "I'm surprised he even knows we're a couple."

"You said he didn't strike you as incompetent," Jace said.

"Did you know Steve Stroud is suffering from dementia?" Rogers asked.

"No." It annoyed Laura that that information had escaped her. "Though it explains why Parker thinks his parents should turn the business over to him now."

"Does he resent his mother's stubbornness enough to try to sabotage the business?" Jace asked.

"Why undermine his own inheritance?" Laura asked. "I think we'd be better off focusing on anyone who has a grudge against the company or the Strouds personally."

"It's possible the bombings and the medication tampering are the work of two different entities," Ramirez said.

"That makes the most sense to me," Jace said. "Poison and bombing are two very different modes of attack. For one thing, the poisoning took out a number of random individuals. The bombing seems more focused."

"Only a handful of people had a key to that door," Rogers said. "The bomb was set to go off when someone inserted their key into the lock."

"But the bomb was planted inside the building," Ramirez said. "Someone would need access to the area on the other side of the door—and time to plant the bomb, probably after everyone left for the day."

"There was only an hour between end of shift and the time of the explosion," Jace said. "They'd need fifteen or twenty minutes at least to be sure the office was empty. We should find out who stayed late that day."

"Or who came back after everyone left," Laura said. "Is there a security camera at that entrance?"

"There was," Rowan said. "It was destroyed in the blast, but maybe the tech guys can pull something off of it."

"Donna mentioned that Gini Elgin's son, Leo, is blaming Stroud Pharmaceuticals for his mother's death," Rogers said. "He could have used Gini's key to let himself into the building after everyone left."

"I saw him here at the factory yesterday," Ramirez said. "At that makeshift memorial on the corner of the property. He smashed a vase full of flowers and looked pretty upset."

"We'll definitely be talking to him." Rogers braced his hands on the back of a chair and leaned toward them. "Ramirez, Cooper and I are going to be talking to every employee over the next few days. But we're counting on you two to figure out what they aren't telling us. Somebody associated with this place has secrets. We learn those, we'll be closer to finding our killer or killers."

THE DAY AFTER the bombing, the factory operated as usual. Jace's job was to monitor a machine that boxed up herbal throat lozenges—twelve bottles of lozenges to each box. He pulled out any boxes that unfolded crookedly or didn't contain twelve bottles. Mistakes didn't happen often, and he had plenty of time to observe the workers around him who monitored various other aspects of the packaging process. Since all the poisoned Stomach Soothers, as well as the missing bottles, were from a single lot, manufactured on a single day, he suspected someone had intercepted the bottles before they were sealed, introduced the ricin in the form of a fine powder that had clung to the tablets, then put the bottles back into the assembly line to proceed to packaging.

How to do that, though, without being noticed?

The woman who was training him, Barb Falk, stopped by two hours into his shift. A stocky middle-aged woman with bleached hair pulled back in a ponytail and sharp blue eyes that didn't appear to miss anything, she was affable and talkative. "How's it going?" she asked.

"No problems so far," he said.

"Yeah, things run pretty smoothly around here," she said. "It can make the job boring at times but be thankful for the boredom. I worked at a place before this where the machinery was always breaking down. We were constantly playing catch-up. Better to sit back and have nothing to do than to constantly be scrambling to do the impossible."

"I can't help thinking about that tragedy with the Stomach Soothers," Jace said. "I heard on a news report that the FBI thinks someone tampered with the tablets before they even left the factory, but I don't see any way that's even possible."

"I guess anything is possible if you try hard enough," she said.

"Being a trainer, you probably know every part of the manufacturing process," Jace said. "How do you think it was done?"

She shook her head. "I don't even go there," she said. "Even if it could be done, why would anyone do it? These are good jobs, hard to come by. Most people who get them really appreciate them." Her eyes met his, her expression daring him to disagree.

"I hear you," he said. "My wife and I feel lucky, getting hired on here. I just hate to think of anyone trying to do something like that, messing everything up for the rest of us."

"If anyone had, they'd be out of here before they knew what hit them," she said.

"Has anyone been fired recently?" he asked.

Her eyes narrowed. "I don't see how that concerns you. Now come on, let's head over to the box sealer. You'll like that one—you actually have to operate the cutter."

He spent the next two hours pressing down on a lever to cut the tape that sealed the top of each box. Not any more exciting than his previous position, but it did require the use of one hand.

He thought about heading upstairs and seeing if Laura wanted to have lunch with him, then thought better of it. Lunch was his best opportunity to interact with his fellow factory workers. While Laura played the role of his wife well enough in public, he didn't sense she relished acting the part more often than necessary.

Still, she wasn't as bad as he had feared she would be. After the first day, she made no complaints about living in a house trailer or giving up her designer clothing. He hadn't been surprised to learn she was a military brat with an accounting degree, but when she had talked about her background he had glimpsed the geeky girl who never lived in one place long enough to make fast friends.

She was an intriguing combination of prickly and soft. It was like she couldn't allow herself to enjoy life. He'd seen that in the military—people so scared of losing control, they clung to the regulations like a lifeline. Do what you're told and you'll be safe.

Except you were never safe. Not really. Obey

all the rules and an IED could still take you out when you were crossing the street. Eat all the right things, do all the right things, and cancer could still show up one day when you least expected it. People like Laura clung to the illusion of control instead of surrendering to the reality that they had none.

She would no doubt be horrified to know he had thought of her that way for even one moment. Smiling to himself at her imagined reaction, he collected his lunch from his locker and made his way to the break room. He sat at a table with some coworkers he recognized, opened the lunch bag and studied the contents. Laura had insisted on making lunch this morning. He had another ham sandwich but with mustard, not mayonnaise, and lettuce, tomato, onion—and was that *cucumber* on top? Instead of chips, he had carrots and celery sticks.

"You don't look too happy with your lunch." The man to his left, whose coveralls identified him as Ed, said.

"My wife's trying to get me to eat healthier." He picked the cucumber slices off the sandwich and set them aside. At least Laura had packed Oreos. For all her love of vegetables, she had a sweet tooth.

"She's the new admin in the office, right?" Phyllis, across from him, asked. "The pretty blonde."

Jace nodded. "Yeah, we were really lucky to both get jobs here. I heard these jobs were hard to come by."

"You came along at the right time," Phyllis said. "They needed someone to fill Benny Cagle's position."

"What happened to Benny Cagle?" Jace took a bite of the ham sandwich. It wasn't bad, but it would have been better with mayo.

"He got fired." Ed crunched down on a grape.

"Why'd he get fired?" Jace asked.

"He had a problem with drugs," Phyllis said. "Heroin."

"I heard it was meth," said a woman down the table.

"No, it was heroin," Phyllis said.

"When was he fired?" Jace asked.

"Oh, I guess it was a couple weeks ago now," Ed said.

"He kept showing up late for work—or not showing up at all," Phyllis said. "Everybody saw it coming, but you can't really talk to someone under the influence, can you?" She shrugged.

"Is he still here in town?" Jace asked.

"I heard he went to live with his sister in Vicksburg," Phyllis said.

"You play softball?" Ed asked Jace.

"Not in a long time," Jace said. "Why?"

"We got a coed team through the local rec

league," Ed said. "You look like you could handle a bat."

"I'll think about it. Thanks." Though, with any luck, he'd be long gone by the time the season was in full swing.

Laura was waiting by the truck when Jace emerged into the parking lot later that afternoon. A soft breeze stirred her hair and fluttered the ruffles along the neck of her blouse. Jace faltered a little, struck by how pretty she looked. Not like the no-nonsense fed he'd come to know.

She spotted him and sent him an annoyed look. He started walking again, not hurrying. She never liked to wait. "How was your day?" he asked as he clicked the key fob to unlock the truck.

She opened the door and swung inside. "I got the name of an employee who was fired just a week ago," she said.

"Yeah. Benny Cagle." He started the truck and turned the air-conditioning up to full.

"Oh. You knew?" There was no hiding her disappointment.

"Some of my coworkers were talking about him at lunch today," Jace said. "They said he got canned for drugs—heroin or meth."

"The official file says he was fired for failing to show up for work and chronic tardiness," she said.

"Easier to prove than drugs," Jace said. "Probably looks better to insurance companies, too."

He glanced at her. "Somebody said he's in Vicksburg, living with his sister."

"We need to make sure he didn't come back to town and plant a bomb," she said.

They spent the rest of the drive to their trailer debating the best way to investigate Cagle. As Jace turned into the driveway, Laura fell silent. Two big cardboard boxes leaned against the steps of the trailer. "What is that?" she asked, tense with wariness.

"That's your new bed." He climbed out of the truck and she followed.

"You ordered a bed delivered?" she asked, eyeing the boxes.

"Sure. Why not?" He examined the boxes then tapped the larger one. "This is the frame." He tapped the other box. "And this is the mattress." She was still frowning, so he added, "You needed a bed. We don't have time to shop."

She met his gaze, her expression softer. "Thank you," she said. "That was very thoughtful of you."

He looked away. She didn't have to act like he'd donated a kidney. "If you'll make dinner, I'll put all this together," he said, gesturing toward the boxes.

Dinner was pasta and chicken in some kind of sauce, which was good, and steamed broccoli—not his favorite, but he ate it because he was hungry. "The pasta is good," he said when they were done.

"It's lemon pepper chicken. I don't cook often," she said. "But I can cook."

"I never said you couldn't." He stood and helped clear the table, then touched her shoulder and turned her toward the door to the rest of the house. "Come see your new bed."

He'd chosen a simple metal frame, antique-looking, and one of those foam mattresses that expanded as soon as you unboxed it. Laura walked around it, surveying it from every angle, then sat on the edge of the mattress.

"How is it?" he asked, immediately annoyed that he cared what she thought.

"Better than the couch."

"That's all you can say?" He sat beside her and gave a little bounce. "Feels pretty good to me. Better than what I've got."

Then he saw the smile tugging at the corner of her mouth. She'd been playing him for sure. She burst out laughing. "It's great, Jace. Thanks."

She looked so pretty when she smiled. Approachable. He leaned toward her, the flowers-and-vanilla scent of her swirling around him. Their eyes met and her lips parted. So inviting…

His phone rang, and they both jumped to their feet. Heart pounding, he fumbled for the phone, avoiding her eyes. What had almost happened there? Whatever it was, it wasn't going to happen again. "Hello," he barked into the phone.

"I'm sending you a report on Leo Elgin," Rogers said. "He's somebody we definitely want to take a closer look at."

"Why?" Jace asked.

"You'll see." Rogers ended the call.

Jace stuffed the phone back in his coveralls. "That was Rogers. He said…"

"I heard." Laura headed for the living room and Jace followed. By the time he reached her, she had her laptop up and running and was accessing the report. "This says Leo Elgin is employed by a firm in Nashville that makes sophisticated security systems for businesses and high-end homes," she said.

"That might give him the skill to create a bomb like the one that went off at the factory. The bomb itself was simple, but the trigger required a little sophistication," Jace said.

"Oh."

The single syllable was freighted with meaning—awe, dismay, interest. "What is it?" he asked and moved in beside her, shoulders brushing.

"Leo Elgin had some trouble in high school," she said. Her eyes met his, reflecting both fear and anger. "He was jailed briefly for giving a bomb to a teacher."

Chapter Five

Six for six.

The three words, bold print in a twenty-point font, stood out on the torn piece of printer paper. "It was in a plain envelope, addressed to me, in this morning's mail." Donna Stroud spoke calmly, only her tightly clenched hands betraying her agitation.

Ana examined the envelope, which she had already placed in a clear evidence pouch. It bore a local postmark, no return address, and had been mailed the day before. The paper that accompanied it looked like plain copy paper, torn in half. "What do you think it means?" Ana asked.

The vertical line between Donna's eyebrows deepened. "Six people died from the tainted Stomach Soothers," she said. "But I don't know what 'six for six' means."

"We'll see if we can get any fingerprints or other evidence from this." Ana slipped the evidence envelopes into her jacket. "Did anyone else in the office see this?"

"Merry Winger puts the mail on my desk, so she probably saw it. She collects it from the mailroom about nine thirty each morning. Someone in the mailroom would have seen it when they sorted it."

"Where can I find Merry?"

"Her desk is just to the left of the door to the outer office. She's the pretty blonde."

Merry was indeed a pretty blonde, all bouncy curls and dramatic eye makeup, including spider-like fake eyelashes. "May I help you?" she asked when Ana approached her desk.

Ana showed her identification. "Do you remember putting this on Mrs. Stroud's desk this morning?" she asked.

Merry leaned forward and studied the envelope in its clear evidence pouch. She wrinkled her nose. "It might have been in with the other mail, but I don't really notice." She sat back and shrugged.

"What's your routine for handling the mail?" Ana asked.

"I go down the hall to the mailroom about nine thirty and collect whatever is in the boxes for this office. Dennis, the mail clerk, sorts everything after the carrier delivers it. I distribute everything for this office. Mrs. Stroud usually has the biggest stack. It used to be Mr. Stroud, but now that he's retired, Mrs. S gets everything that isn't addressed to accounting or personnel or a specific person."

"So you would have sorted this letter into the stack to go to Mrs. Stroud?"

"Well, yeah, but I just toss anything that isn't for anyone else into her pile. I don't stop and read anything or pay much attention." She leaned forward again, eyes bright with interest. "Why? Is that letter from the bomber?"

"Why do you think it might be from the bomber?" Ana asked.

"Well, duh! You're from the FBI, and you've got that envelope all sealed up in that pouch. If it was junk mail you wouldn't treat it that way."

"We don't know who the letter is from," Ana said. "I'm trying to find out."

"Sorry, I can't help you," Merry said.

"If you think of anything, let me know." Ana handed her card to the young woman and headed to the mail room, where Dennis told her he hadn't noticed anything unusual about the letter either.

Back at the situation room at the local police department that she and Rogers were using as their workspace, Rogers examined the letter and envelope. "'Six for six,'" he said. "A reference to the six people who were killed by the poisoned Stomach Soothers?"

"Donna Stroud thinks so." Ana studied the three words. "Maybe the bomber is saying he—

or she—plans to kill six people in retaliation for the six who died."

"Kill as in set more bombs?"

"We don't know, do we?" She sank into one of the rolling desk chairs the local police had provided them. "People are poisoned and someone responds by planting a bomb. Where's the logic in that?"

"It makes sense to the bomber—our job is to get into his head and figure out how."

"Leo Elgin made it clear he blamed the Strouds for killing his mother," Ana said. "He has the skills to build a bomb and a history of making a bomb threat. It shows us he thinks of a bomb as a weapon."

Rogers nodded. "It's past time we talked to Leo."

"THE BOMB I gave Mrs. Pepper wasn't real," Leo said. "It was just a bunch of highway flares taped together and wired to a clock. Anyone with sense would have seen right away it was a fake. Which was the whole point, because Mrs. Pepper didn't have any sense."

Leo Elgin stared across the table at Ana, deep shadows beneath his eyes like smudges of soot, his hair falling listlessly across his pale forehead. He wore the same T-shirt and jeans he had had on when she had seen him at the memorial Sunday outside the Stroud plant, and the sour smell of his body odor hung in the air around him.

"Why did you give your teacher a fake bomb?" Ana asked.

"Because she was an idiot and I wanted to prove it. She freaked out about a bomb that looked like something out of a cartoon."

"But you were the one who got into trouble." Rogers moved from where he had been leaning against the wall to loom over Elgin, his muscular bulk making the young man look even smaller. "You were expelled from school." The school district had eventually dropped the charges and Leo had been released from jail. It had taken some serious digging to uncover the incident.

Leo jutted out his lower lip like a pouting adolescent. "I hated the place anyway. It was full of idiots."

"Was Parker Stroud an idiot?" Rogers asked.

Something flickered across Leo's face—confusion? Fear? "Parker was okay," he said.

Ana leaned toward him. "Were you and Parker friends?" she asked.

"No, we weren't friends."

"But you knew him."

His nostrils flared as he blew out a breath. "We had, like, thirty people in our whole class. Everybody knew everybody. But it's not like we hung out or anything."

"Why didn't the school press charges against you?" Ana asked.

"Haven't you been listening? It wasn't a real bomb."

"You can be charged for threatening someone, even if your threat isn't real," Rogers said. "With all the incidents of school violence, how did you ever think you'd get away with such a stupid stunt?"

Leo flinched at the word "stupid," as if Rogers had slapped him. "People around here knew me. They knew I wasn't dangerous."

"Your mother worked for the Strouds," Ana said. "Maybe the Strouds put in a good word for you. After all, their business is the biggest employer in town. They probably had a lot of influence."

Leo's scowl turned ugly. "I didn't need the Strouds to pull any strings for me."

"Do you blame the Strouds for your mother's death?" Rogers asked.

A flash of anger this time. Leo sat up straighter. "They're responsible. The medication they make killed her. If they had any kind of quality control this wouldn't have happened."

"Your mother died." Rogers's voice was flat. Cold. "You held the Strouds responsible. So you decided to make them pay."

A sharp jerk of his head, left to right. "They'll

pay," he said. "I've already talked to a lawyer. She thinks I have a good case."

"A bomb is quicker," Rogers said.

Leo's face twisted. "Look, I wouldn't do that. I knew Lydia. She was a nice person." His voice broke. "She and my mom were friends." He covered his eyes with one hand.

Rogers braced his hands on the table next to Leo. "We're going to search your mother's house, your car, and your apartment and office in Nashville," he said. "If you made that bomb, we're going to find out."

"Go ahead and look." Leo lowered his hand. "You won't find anything."

"How long do you plan to stay in Mayville?" Ana asked.

"Why? Are you going to tell me not to leave town?"

"Answer the question," Rogers said. "How long do you plan to be in town?"

Leo slumped in the chair. "I don't know. The… the service for my mother is Saturday, but then I need to decide what to do with the house and… I don't know. I can't really think of anything right now."

"When do you have to be back at work at Integrated Security?" Ana asked.

"I took a leave of absence. My boss said I could come back when I'm ready." His eyes met hers. The anguish in them was like a raw wound. "She was all I had—my mother. It was just her and me, all those years. I don't know what I'm going to do without her."

Rogers moved away, toward the door. "You can go now, but we'll be in touch," he said.

When he was gone, Ana and Rogers moved to the room next door, where Smitty and Cantrell had been observing through the one-way glass. "Good call on asking about Parker Stroud," Cantrell said. "That got a reaction from him."

"It was a reaction," Rogers agreed. "I just don't know what it means."

"His grief was real," Ana said. "I think he's seriously depressed."

"I agree," Rogers said. "But that just gives him more of a motivation for wanting to harm the Strouds."

"Do you think the Strouds really persuaded the school not to press charges over that fake bomb?" Smitty asked.

Rogers shrugged. "It makes sense. His mother was a key employee, close to the same age as the Strouds. She probably went to them for help and they leaned on the school to get them to agree to not press charges, provided Leo transferred to another school."

"His mom sent him to a military academy for a year," Ana said, referring to her notes.

"That didn't come cheap," Cantrell said. "I

wouldn't be surprised if the Strouds paid for that, too."

"If he owes the Strouds so much, why blame them for his mother's death?" Smitty asked.

"Maybe because he owes them so much," Cantrell said. "Obligation carries its own weight."

"You heard him," Rogers said. "Everyone at school was an idiot. His teacher was an idiot. Elgin thinks he's the smartest man in the room, whatever the room."

"Maybe he thinks he's smart enough to get away with planting a real bomb at the Stroud factory," Cantrell said.

"That bomb wasn't planted at a factory entrance," Smitty said. "It was wired to a door only office personnel used. Only a few people had a key that would trigger the detonation."

"Which brings us back to the Strouds," Ana said. "Donna, Steve and Parker all have keys."

"And Leo probably has Gini Elgin's key," Smitty said.

"The local police already searched her house," Rogers said. "They didn't find the key, or any bomb-making materials."

"We need to monitor his phone and computer usage," Cantrell said. "If he built that bomb, he had to get the materials from somewhere."

"Did his mother have a storage unit anywhere near here?" Smitty asked. "Maybe he's keeping the materials there."

"We haven't found anything yet," Rogers said. He pointed to Cantrell. "I'll see about getting permission to bug his place and monitor his computer."

"Let me know when you're ready," Cantrell said. He was the team's specialist in electronic surveillance.

"Have you two come up with anything yet?" Rogers asked.

Smitty shook her head. "Not yet."

"We checked out the fired employee, Benny Cagle," Ana said. "He was in jail in Vicksburg, Mississippi, where he had been living with his sister, when the bombing occurred."

"Had been since before the Stomach Soother tablets were poisoned," Rogers said.

"Do we think the crimes are related?" Smitty asked. "Are we looking for one person or two?"

"Seems a big coincidence to have two crimes like this centered around one small-town business, so close together," Cantrell said.

"But two very different crimes," Smitty said. "So maybe two different people with similar motivations."

"What's the motivation?" Rogers asked.

"I don't know yet." She shook her head. "We need to dig deeper with the Strouds. Maybe they're hiding something."

"Everybody is hiding something," Cantrell

said. "The question is whether their secrets are relevant to our investigation."

They tossed around more theories for a few minutes, then the meeting broke up. Ana and Smitty headed for the ladies' room. "How are things going with you and Jace?" Ana asked when she and Smitty were washing their hands at the row of sinks.

Smitty grimaced. "It's okay. At least I'm not sleeping on the couch anymore."

"Oh?" Ana didn't even try to hide her surprise.

Smitty flushed. "I mean, I have a bed now. There was only one when we moved in, and Jace took it."

"How gentlemanly of him."

Smitty waved aside the comment. "He's a lot taller than I am, so it made sense to stick me with the couch. I got the best revenge, though. My new bed is supposedly a lot more comfortable than the old one he's sleeping on."

Ana dug a tube of lipstick from her bag. "Things are going okay, then. Better than you expected?"

"Yeah. I guess so." Smitty combed her fingers through her long hair.

"For what it's worth, you two look good together." Ana studied her fellow agent in the mirror. "Like a real couple."

"Who would have guessed we were such good actors?" But Smitty's cheeks were still pink, and there was a brightness in her eyes Ana hadn't seen before. Ana smiled. She liked Smitty. She was a good agent, but maybe a little too tightly wound sometimes. Cantrell might change that.

"What are you smiling about?" Rogers asked when Ana rejoined him.

"I was thinking Smitty and Cantrell might make a good couple."

"No way! Those two are like oil and water. I'm surprised they've been able to live in that trailer for more than one night without coming to blows."

"They're professionals." But they were human, too. The job was only one aspect of their lives. She thought of her fiancé, Benning Reeves, and his two children. The four of them would soon be a family. Knowing that added meaning to her work.

"Cantrell and Smitty will both be glad when this case is over," Rogers said.

Maybe, Ana thought. And maybe she was being overly romantic, seeing a match for those two. But stranger things had happened in this line of work.

JACE PUT A hand at Laura's back as they walked across the parking lot from the police station. She forced herself not to shrug it off. It was the kind of gesture a husband might make to his wife and fit their cover. Truth be told, she didn't really want to shrug him off. The weight of his hand was warm and pleasant—almost comforting. "Some of the guys at the plant were telling me about a lake south of town," he said. "We should check it out."

"Why? Does it have something to do with the case?"

"I just thought it would be someplace nice to see. You know, to relax."

They reached the truck, he unlocked it, and they climbed in.

"All right." Though she felt anything but relaxed around this man. She was so hyperaware of him—of his bulk filling the driver's seat of the truck, the muscles in his forearm tensing as he shifted gears, the sweet scent of the cinnamon gum he chewed.

"Why do you always chew gum?" she asked.

He glanced at her. "Does it bother you?"

She shrugged. "I just wondered."

"I quit smoking six months ago. I guess you could say I traded a nicotine habit for a gum habit."

"Good for you."

"Yeah, well, I still miss it. It's just damned inconvenient when I'm working. Did you ever smoke?"

She shook her head.

"Yeah, I should have guessed."

"What is that supposed to mean?"

"You're like those girls I knew in high school— the ones who didn't drink or smoke or swear or skip school or so much as jaywalk. They always looked perfect and spoke perfect and acted perfect."

"And you didn't want anything to do with them," she said.

"Oh no. You've got it all wrong." He shook his head. "Those girls were untouchable. And I wanted so bad to touch them, to make them feel. To help them discover the bad girl I knew had to be hiding inside that pristine shell."

The rich velvet of his voice and the teasing words sent a quiver through her, low in the belly. She had been one of those girls, the ones too afraid to ever break the rules. He was the kind of boy she would have shunned, too terrified of the things he might make her feel.

She was a woman now, one with enough experience that men like him no longer frightened her. Or so she told herself.

Neither of them spoke on the rest of the drive to the lake. Laura leaned back in the seat and closed her eyes, reviewing the interview with Leo Elgin, trying to sort out where his evidence fit with everything else they knew about this case.

The silver-blue expanse of the lake reflected the pines that crowded the shore on three sides, with a rough sand beach bordered by picnic tables nearest the lot where they parked. Only half a dozen other vehicles shared space in the big lot. "They must get crowds here on the weekends, with a parking lot this size," Laura observed as she and Jace climbed out of the pickup truck.

"I'll bet a lot of high school kids come here at night to make out and party," Jace said. "At least, that's what I would have done."

Yes, Jace had probably been many a father's worst nightmare in high school. "Did you ever do that?" he asked. "Sneak out to the park and party with your friends—or make out with your boyfriend, music playing low on the radio, the moon shining down?"

He made it sound so carefree and romantic. "My father was a lieutenant colonel," she said. "And we usually lived on base."

"So no guy had the guts to risk sneaking around with you," Jace said.

"I guess." She wouldn't admit to Jace that she was the one who hadn't had the courage to defy her father.

They took a path that circled the lake. The earthy smell of sun-warmed weeds and lake water mingled with the heavier perfume of honeysuckle. Laura breathed in deeply, feeling some of the tension of the day easing from her shoulders. "This was a good idea," she said. "It's relaxing."

"It's the water," he said. "I read a study that says water relaxes us because it syncs up with our brain waves or something."

She laughed. "That's your scientific explanation—or something?"

He shrugged. "I don't have to understand why being around water eases stress. I'm just glad it does." He scooped a rock from the shore and sent it skipping across the glassy surface of the water—one, two, three, four times, concentric circles spreading out and colliding to form mesmerizing patterns. He moved with the grace of a boy—and the bunching muscles and sinewy strength of a man. Being with him made Laura so much more aware of herself not only as a fellow agent, but also as a woman.

What was wrong with her? she wondered. She had worked with other men before, and she had never been attracted to any of them. Maybe that was because she always put the job first and didn't allow herself to focus on anything else.

Why was being with Jace so different?

"When I was a kid, for four or five years in a row, we went to a lake house on vacation," Jace said, as they continued on the path. "The place was just a little cabin, nothing fancy at all, but we loved it. We fished and paddled around in a canoe or swam off the dock. In the evenings, my dad would build a fire and we'd roast hot dogs or cook burgers in packets of foil, or even fish we'd caught. Looking back, I realize that for my folks, it was probably a really cheap vacation, but my sister and I loved it so much. I think we would have chosen that little lake house over a big amusement park. At least I know I would have."

"My parents sent me to a girl's camp in upstate New York one summer," Laura said. "Two weeks in a cabin with six other girls and six hundred spiders. I got poison ivy the third day, made a lanyard that was all knots, and almost shot my bunkmate in the head during archery practice."

"Good times," Jace said, and she laughed—a full belly laugh she couldn't keep back.

"Let's just say my first experience camping didn't make me want to try again," she said.

"I bet you'd be good at it now," he said.

"What makes you think that?" She genuinely wanted to know.

"Because you're not a whiner. And you're practical. You assess what needs to be done and you do it. Those are great strengths for camping."

"Who knew camping was so much like an investigation?" Their eyes met and her heart stuttered in its rhythm. When Jace looked at her, she felt as if he was really seeing her—all of her. She didn't like feeling so exposed, even if the heat behind his look told her he liked what he saw.

He was the first to look away, however. He frowned over her shoulder. "Isn't that Parker Stroud?" he asked.

She turned, moving slowly, as if she was merely brushing something from her shoulder, and glanced across the parking lot. Parker Stroud, dressed casually in jeans and a blue polo shirt, a West Virginia Mountaineers ball cap tugged down on his forehead, was striding away from a sleek black pickup truck. "That's him," she said.

"Let's go see what he's up to."

Keeping a line of trees between themselves and Parker, they trailed him to a fishing pier that jutted thirty feet out into the lake. He stood, looking out over the water, hands clasped behind his back. "He's waiting for someone," Laura said.

"Maybe he comes out here to look at the water because it's relaxing," Jace said.

"Then why doesn't he look more relaxed?"

Parker turned to glance toward the parking lot. Jace and Laura shrank further into the shadows as a slight figure in jeans and a gray hoodie slouched across the lot toward the pier. Laura studied the new arrival. Something about him was very familiar. "I think that's Leo Elgin," she whispered.

"Maybe," Jace said. "He changed clothes."

"He had time to do that."

The two men stood a couple of feet apart, Parker with his arms crossed tightly over his chest, Leo with his hands on his hips. Jace and Laura were too far away to hear the conversation, but the men's postures and expressions didn't appear friendly. Parker started shaking his head emphatically, and then Leo abruptly turned and fled.

Laura moved back through the trees toward the parking lot, following Leo, while Jace stayed to watch Parker. But by the time she reached the parking lot, all she could see was a pair of tail-lights receding into the distance.

Her cell phone buzzed and she read the text from Jace letting her know Parker was headed her way. She took cover behind a van and watched while Parker stalked to his truck, got in and drove off.

Jace jogged up to Laura. "Anything else happen?" he asked.

"Leo drove out of here before I could even get his plate number," she said. "The way he raced out of here, I'd say he was pretty upset."

"Leo blames the Strouds for killing his mother," Jace said. "Maybe he followed Parker here to have it out with him about that."

"Parker manages the manufacturing facilities at Stroud," Laura said. "So Leo may see him as being most responsible for the poisoned Stomach Soother tablets."

"It's not illegal to have a conversation," Jace said. "And they've never denied knowing each other."

"No." She turned back toward their truck. "But I think this wasn't a chance meeting. I think Parker was waiting for Leo."

"We need to find out what they were talking about," Jace said. "But we need to do it without blowing our cover."

"I'll see what I can get out of Parker," she said. Though, considering Stroud's generally surly attitude, that wouldn't be an easy task.

Chapter Six

Parker Stroud didn't appear in his office until almost noon the next day. He strode past Laura's desk without a glance in her direction and shut his door firmly behind him. Laura decided to wait to pass on the half-dozen messages that had come in his absence—two of them from his mother, who hadn't sounded too happy that her son hadn't shown up for work yet.

Ten minutes later, Laura's phone lit up. "I need hard copies of all the quality control reports for the first quarter," he said, and hung up before she could reply.

Since she had spent the morning continuing her search through the files, both online and off, Laura had no trouble locating the reports, though she wondered why Parker didn't pull them up on his computer. She spent the next half hour printing and collating the reports, which were submitted twice a week. Scanning the documents as she worked, she saw nothing that raised alarms. Stroud Pharmaceuticals had apparently been meticulous about maintaining quality control. So how had the ricin gotten into those tablets?

She knocked on Parker's door and, when he barked "Come in," slipped inside.

"Here are the reports," she said, laying the papers on his blotter. "And your messages." She added the stack of While You Were Out slips.

He grunted, focused on the screen of his desktop computer. After a moment, he finally looked at her. "What do you want?" he asked.

I want to know what you and Leo Elgin were talking about last night, she thought, but said, "Do you need anything else?"

"When I need something from you, I'll ask."

Yeah, getting anything out of this guy was going to be tough. She turned to go. "Laura?"

She stopped and faced him. "Yes?"

"What did the FBI ask you yesterday?"

"If we knew anything about the explosion. We didn't."

"You can't blame them for being suspicious. You and your husband are the only new people around here."

"I guess you knew the woman who was killed?"

The lines around his eyes tightened. "Yes."

"I always thought it would be nice, growing up in a small town where you knew everyone," she said. "But when something like this happens, I guess it makes it harder."

"Yes."

"Do you have any idea who planted that bomb?" she asked. "Who would want to do something so horrible?"

"No. Why are you so interested, anyway?"

"It's such a horrible thing. Especially after the poisonings."

"Maybe you don't want to work at such a horrible place. If you keep asking so many nosy questions, I think that could be arranged."

She backed out of the room, biting her lip to keep from making an angry retort. The phone rang as she was crossing to her desk. "Hello again, Laura." Donna Stroud had a pleasant voice, though Laura didn't miss the weariness underlying her words. "Has Parker made it in yet?"

"Yes ma'am. He came in a little while ago."

"Put me through to him, please."

Laura transferred the call. She debated listening in on the conversation, but before she could pick up the receiver again, Parker's voice sounded through the door, loud and clear. "I'm taking care of it, Mother. I'm not some idiot you have to micromanage... I put in plenty of hours for this company. If I want to come in late one morning, I can."

The receiver slammed down and seconds later Laura's intercom sounded. "Get me hard copies of the first quarter production reports."

"For which factory?"

"All of them!"

She hung up the phone and frowned at Parker's closed door. Was he trying to inundate her with busywork? Why would he need all these reports?

Unless, maybe, he wanted to share them with someone else—someone he couldn't merely forward computer links to.

JACE WAS WORKING the filling line today, monitoring the machinery that was calibrated to inject exactly .70 milliliters of solution into each bottle of Stroud's Soothing Eye Drops. No one spoke to him as he worked, or even looked at him directly, though he could feel the furtive glances of his coworkers. Word had probably gotten around that the FBI had questioned the new guy, and they were all wondering if he was responsible for the bomb that had killed Lydia Green.

Jace pretended not to notice the cold shoulder and concentrated on studying the manufacturing process, trying to spot the weak points in the system, where the poisoner might have introduced the ricin without being seen.

Even with the investigation to occupy his mind, the work was beyond boring. How did his coworkers stand it? He was all too aware that if he had stayed in his hometown, this would have been his lot. It was either that or the coal mines. Or the military. The army had been his ticket out—that and the education the army had paid for. Most of the people he had graduated high school with had opted to stay close to home and take what had looked like good jobs to them. Now the mines were shutting down and half the factories were shipping jobs overseas.

His sister's husband had been laid off so many times he had stopped looking for work.

Jobs like the one Jace was doing now were coveted in a place like Mayville. He had a hard time believing an employee would do anything to jeopardize them, but experience had taught him that people's motives for wrongdoing weren't always logical.

The time arrived for his mandatory break and he headed for the coffee machine. The quartet of fellow workers already in the break room ignored him as he entered, continuing their conversation. "I saw Leo at Bundy's Place night before last," an older man with a pockmarked face said.

"What were you doing at Bundy's Place?" a redhead with pink glasses asked.

"Hey, they have a great happy hour," the man said.

"Tonight is catfish night," a second man said. "There'll be a full house."

"Do you think Leo will be there?" a woman with her hair in braids asked. "I'd like to see him, and tell him how sorry I was about his mom."

"The bartender is a friend of mine," the first man said. "He told me Leo has been there every night. Drowning his sorrows, I guess."

"Miss Gini wouldn't be happy about that," Pink Glasses said.

"She wouldn't be happy about a lot of things that are happening around here lately."

The conversation ended as Barb entered the room. Her gaze slid over the group, then fixed on Jace. "Well?" she asked.

Jace tossed his half-drunk coffee into the trash. "Well, what?"

"Well, did you have anything to do with that bomb?"

The others stared at him, mixed fear and anger on their grim faces.

"No," Jace said. "My wife and I came here to work, not to cause trouble."

"The FBI didn't arrest you," Pink Glasses said. "I guess if they thought you were guilty, you wouldn't be here now."

"Maybe the feds are watching, gathering evidence," Pockmarked Face said.

"They won't find any evidence against me," Jace said. "And why would I want to bomb the place where I'd only worked a day? I didn't even know the poor woman who died."

"Some people are just mean," the woman with the braids said.

Jace couldn't argue with that statement. He had met plenty of mean people in his life. But even mean people usually had a motive behind their meanness. It might be a misguided or completely unfounded motive, but in their minds it justified their meanness. Figuring out the motives behind the sabotage of Stroud Pharmaceuticals would go a long way toward finding the person responsible.

By the end of his shift, a few people had loosened up around Jace. But he was no closer to figuring out how the ricin had gotten into those tablets.

He was waiting for Laura at the truck when she emerged from the front offices. "How did it go?" he asked.

"Parker was in a foul mood," she said. "He didn't come in until noon, and then he spent the rest of the day keeping me running with busywork. I couldn't find any way to bring up Leo's name, much less the meeting at the park. What about you?"

"At least some of my coworkers no longer think I'm the mad bomber." He started the truck, the old engine rumbling roughly to life. "Let's go out tonight."

She blinked. "What? Why?"

"We're going out. To a place called Bundy's. I hear they have good catfish."

She wrinkled her nose. "Let me guess—it's fried."

"Of course."

She turned her head to gaze out the window. "I don't know if I want to go."

Did that translate to *I don't want to eat fried*

fish, or *I don't want to go anywhere with you*? Probably both. Too bad. She was stuck with him for the duration. "You do want to go," he said. "It's where Leo Elgin has been drowning his sorrows every night this week."

She whipped her head back around. "Catfish it is, then."

BUNDY'S PLACE WAS a tin-roofed, windowless barn of a building at the intersection of two county roads five miles out of Mayville. Ancient oaks shaded the building, and the bass thump from a three-piece band reverberated across the parking lot which, by the time Laura and Jace arrived, was packed with cars and pickup trucks.

The smell of beer and frying fish perfumed the air as they stepped inside. They found a table with a view of the bar and Jace went to get drinks. He came back with two beers.

The beer was so cold it made her teeth hurt, but it tasted refreshing. She scanned the crowd, spotting several familiar faces from the plant. "I don't see Leo," she said.

"It's early yet." A waitress arrived to take their order and the tables around them began to fill. A few minutes later, their server returned, bearing two baskets full of catfish, fries and coleslaw. Laura stared at the food, suddenly ravenous. "Go ahead," Jace said. "It won't bite back."

The fish was tender and meaty, the cornmeal

coating crispy and spicy, and not at all greasy. She didn't know when she had eaten something so delicious.

The band, which had taken a break, began playing again, an upbeat country song she recognized from the radio. Jace shoved back his chair and stood. "Let's dance," he said.

"We're supposed to be here spying on Leo Elgin," she reminded him.

"He hasn't shown up yet." He leaned over and tugged on her hand. "Shame to waste the evening."

She let him lead her onto the already crowded dance floor. She couldn't remember the last time she had danced, but Jace made it easy, guiding her through steps she thought she had forgotten, and even leading her through a few new moves. It was a heady feeling, being twirled around the dance floor by a capable partner.

The music changed to a slow ballad. Laura turned to leave the dance floor, but Jace pulled her close. He looked into her eyes, one brow quirked in silent question. *Why not?*

She settled against him. Being so close to him felt dangerous—and thrilling. She let herself enjoy the feel of his arm encircling her lightly, his hand clasping hers. The music was slow and dreamy. Sexy. She closed her eyes, feeling the music wash over her, breathing in the hint of cinnamon that always clung to him and leaning into his embrace. When she opened her eyes, he was looking at her, a raw longing in his gaze that made her breath catch and her heart beast faster. She tried to look away, only to shift her gaze to his lips, the pull of them impossible to resist. The song ended and she let the kiss come, his mouth firm and insistent, her body pressed against his.

A loud whistle, followed by laughter, broke the spell. She stared up at Jace, who looked amused now, and heat flooded her cheeks. Backing away, she hurried off the dance floor to the ladies' room, where she sat in a stall, trying to catch her breath and pull herself together. She and Jace were supposed to be working together. They were professionals, yet they had just behaved very unprofessionally.

You're human, a small voice inside of her whispered—one she didn't listen to very often. She wasn't going to listen to it now.

When she was feeling more composed, she emerged from the stall, washed her hands and studied her face in the scratched mirror. She looked the same as always—a little pale, maybe, but calm. Competent. Not the type of woman who would get involved with a coworker on an assignment.

But what did that kind of woman look like, anyway?

She left the ladies' room, almost colliding with a man in the hallway. He mumbled an apology and brushed past, head down, but not before she had gotten a good look at him. She hurried back to their table, where Jace was accepting an order of two fresh beers from their waitress.

"You didn't have to run off," he said as she settled into the chair beside him. "But hey, I'm sorry if—"

She waved away the apology and leaned toward him, keeping her voice low. "I just saw Leo Elgin," she said.

"Where?"

"He was headed into the men's room." She swiveled in her chair to get a view of the hallway that led to the restrooms.

"There he is," Jace said as Leo merged with the crowd, moving toward the bar. Jace tapped her shoulder. "You go talk to him."

Laura made her way to the bar, hanging back until the chair next to Leo was vacated. She slipped up beside him and when he glanced her way, she stuck out her hand. "Hi, I'm Laura," she said. "I'm new in town. Are you from around here?"

He looked down at his drink. "I'm not exactly good company right now. Maybe you should find someone else to talk to."

"Oh, what's wrong?" She leaned toward him. "If you want to talk about it, people tell me I'm a good listener. Sometimes it helps to get things off your chest, you know?"

"Talking won't help this." He took a long pull of his beer. "My mother died a week ago. She was murdered."

Laura gasped. "That's horrible! Who killed her? Do they know?"

He studied her, eyes narrowed. "She was one of the people who died after taking poisoned Stroud's Stomach Soother tablets."

"I'm so sorry." Laura lightly touched his shoulder. "That is just horrible. I heard about that on TV. Actually, I just went to work at Stroud. I wasn't so sure about the job, after what happened with those Stomach Soothers and everything, but I really needed the money, you know?"

"You work in the plant?" Leo asked.

"No, I'm in the office. I'm Parker Stroud's secretary."

Leo's eyes widened and he set his beer down with a thump. "Do you know Mr. Stroud?" Laura asked.

He looked away. "I know him a little."

"I'll admit, as a boss he's a little intimidating."

"Parker is all right. He's pretty torn up about what happened."

"Oh? You've spoken to him recently?"

"No. I just... I just know he's that kind of guy."

"I think if I was in your place, the Strouds wouldn't be my favorite people right now," she said. "I mean, aren't they supposed to have safety rules and stuff to keep that kind of thing from happening?"

"Yeah, but Parker's mom and dad really run the place. They won't let him modernize the way he wants. He thinks he could have prevented this."

That was interesting. Were things really more lax than she and Jace suspected? Was Parker asking for all the safety and production reports in order to make a case for changes?

"Fight!" A roar rose up from the crowd behind them and she and Leo turned in time to see a chair sail through the air and crash against a pillar. Two men were grappling, rolling on the floor, fists flying.

"Jace!" Laura screamed the name as she recognized one of the men on the floor—who currently had blood streaming down his face.

Chapter Seven

Jace knew trouble was headed his way the minute he saw the look in the man's eye. He just didn't have enough time to get out of the way. "Are you Jace Lovejoy?" the man—six-foot-four with eighteen-inch biceps—asked.

"Who's asking?" Jace stood, hands on the table, out where the man could see them.

"My name is Shay Green and my aunt was Lydia Green. Somebody told me the cops think you planted that bomb that killed her."

"I had nothing to do with that bomb," Jace said. "And I'm sorry about your—"

But he never finished the sentence. Green's fist was already headed his way. Jace ducked, and flipped the table at Green, throwing him off balance long enough for Jace to step up and land a blow that should have ended the fight before it started.

But Green—hyped-up on grief and adrenaline and the alcohol that came off of him in fumes—hadn't gotten the memo. He momentarily staggered under the force of the blow, then charged at Jace like an enraged bull.

The next thing Jace knew, he was on the floor with blood streaming from his nose and Green straddling his chest. Someone else tried to pull Green off of him and Jace took advantage of the distraction to squirm out from under him and knee him in the chin. Green's howl hurt his ears and he dove at Jace again.

They rolled across the floor, into tables, dodging people's feet. Jace would be on top, then Green. A circle of spectators had formed around them by the time they got to their feet again, grappling in the clumsy way of two evenly matched fighters, neither of whom would give an inch.

"The cops are on their way!" someone shouted, and Jace swore under his breath. He didn't want to have to explain this to the local police and risk blowing his cover. He shoved Green back. "You got the wrong guy!" he yelled. "Leave me alone."

In answer, Green punched him in the gut. Jace doubled over, fighting for breath, vision going gray. Two men dragged Green back, and Jace felt a hand on his back. He whirled, fist raised, to face Laura. She wrapped both hands around his arm and dragged him toward the edge of the crowd. "Come on," she said. "We've got to get out of here."

He didn't try to resist, but let her lead him through the crowd and out a side door to the parking lot. He was dazed and bleeding, and only when he felt her hand digging in his pants pocket did he wake up. "What are you doing?" he asked.

"I need the keys to the truck."

He pushed her hand away and fished out the keys. "Come on," she said, taking the keys and grabbing hold of his arm again.

They turned out of the parking lot just as the first patrol car turned in. Jace leaned back in the seat, eyes closed, trying not to think about how much his face hurt. "What was that all about?" Laura asked.

"He said he was Lydia Green's nephew." Jace's voice sounded thick and unfamiliar. "He was drunk and had it in his head that I was responsible for the bomb that killed his aunt."

"But a fight? What were you thinking? What if you had had to draw your weapon?"

Jace was very aware of the gun holstered out of sight at his ankle. "I wouldn't have shot the guy."

"What if he had threatened you with a gun?" she asked.

"That didn't happen. He used his fists." He gingerly touched his nose and winced. "He could have broken my nose."

She braked hard, throwing him forward against the seat belt. "Do we need to go to the doctor? The hospital?"

"I don't think my nose is broken. I just need to get back to the trailer and clean up." He shifted to dig a handkerchief from his pocket and pressed it to his still-bleeding nose. "What did you find out from Elgin?"

"He says Parker's parents are preventing Parker from modernizing the factory. I got the impression he blames Donna and Steve, but not Parker, for what happened to his mother."

"The two of them didn't look all that friendly when we saw them at the lake yesterday."

"No, and Leo didn't really talk about Parker as if they were best buddies. But he did talk as if he knew him well—as if maybe they had been closer once." She had detected a note of regret in Leo's voice when he spoke about Parker.

"Maybe Leo was confronting Parker about Leo's mother's death and he was angry Parker wasn't pressing his parents to do more," Jace said.

"Or maybe there's no way we'll ever know what they talked about unless they tell us." Laura turned the truck into the rutted drive to the trailer. She parked and climbed out, but Jace was slower to join her. He moved stiffly, as if in pain. "What's wrong?" she asked. "Did he hurt more than your nose?"

"I'm still feeling a couple of those punches." Jace tried to straighten, but grimaced and remained bent over.

Laura took his arm. "Come on. I think there's a first aid kit in the closet."

"Nothing a stiff whiskey and a good night's sleep won't cure."

She wanted to lecture him on the stupidity of fighting. If things had turned ugly and he'd had to pull his weapon to defend himself, their cover would have been blown and the operation aborted. Not to mention, he could have been seriously injured, and she'd have been without a partner. While Jace went into the bathroom to wash off as much blood as possible, she rummaged through shelves until she found the first aid kit. When he emerged, water still dripping from the ends of his hair, purpling bruises already forming beneath both eyes, she had an assortment of bandages and ointments laid out on the kitchen table.

"Are you sure your nose isn't broken?" she asked, eyeing him critically.

"I'm sure." He squeezed the tip between his thumb and forefinger, wincing as he did so. "I couldn't stand that if it was. But he did bang it up pretty good."

"At least put some antibiotic ointment on that cut on your lip and the one on your chin," she said. "He must have been wearing a big ring or something."

"Everything about the dude was big."

"I hope he doesn't decide to come after you again."

"I'm touched that you're so concerned for me," he said as he dabbed ointment onto his chin.

"I'm concerned for me. We live together."

His eyes met hers, and she felt that flare of heat again, the spark that seemed to ignite every time they were alone together. "About that kiss on the dance floor," he began.

"I don't want to talk about that kiss."

"We need to talk about the kiss." He reached out and captured her hand in his.

"It shouldn't have happened," she said, trying, and failing, to pull away from him. "It was a momentary lapse of judgment."

"I think it was the natural reaction of a man and a woman who are attracted to each other."

"We are work partners. Gender shouldn't figure into it."

"We're human beings, not robots. Gender is part of what makes us who we are." He rubbed his thumb across her knuckles, sending a current of sensation through her, like an electrical charge. "I'm pretty happy about that right now."

She jerked her hand away from him. "We have a job to do," she said. "We can't make this about us."

He straightened in his chair. "I respect your feelings, even though I think you're wrong. If you really believe the only way to handle this is to keep things strictly business between us, then I'll do that."

She forced herself to look him in the eye again. "I have to know that I can trust you," she said.

His expression hardened. "I never have and I never will force myself on a woman. You don't have to worry about anything like that."

"I didn't mean..." But what had she meant? Maybe it wasn't Jace she couldn't trust but herself when she was around him. He made her forget the woman she needed to be in favor of a wilder, more out-of-control version of herself. Losing herself that way felt more dangerous than any criminal she had ever faced.

Laura drove to work the next morning while Jace, his face an ugly mass of bruises, sat hunched over in the passenger seat. "Maybe you should have called in sick," she said.

"Everyone will have heard about the fight by now. If I don't show up for work, they'll think Green got the best of me."

"It looks to me like he did," she said.

He glared at her, which only made her grin. Grumpy Jace was certainly easier to handle than easygoing Jace, who always seemed to find a way to glide past her doubts and hesitations.

That wasn't quite a fair assessment, of course. True to his word, he hadn't so much as brushed up against her this morning, keeping a very respectful and businesslike distance between them and coming to the breakfast table this morning fully and properly dressed.

What did it say about her that she had spent half the meal picturing him without his shirt anyway?

She was on her way to her office when Donna Stroud intercepted her. "Laura, I was hoping I'd catch you," she said. "Could I speak with you in my office for a minute?"

Laura followed the older woman into her office. Donna settled heavily into the chair behind her desk. She looked as if she had aged in the last week, the lines around her eyes and on either side of her mouth deepened. "Is something wrong?" Laura asked.

"I'm hoping you can tell me if you've made any progress in this case," Donna said.

"I don't have anything I can share with you at this time," Laura said. They had one suspect for the bombing and nothing for the poisoning, and things were moving agonizingly slow. "Investigations like this take time," she continued. "There's a lot of evidence to sift through and people to question." Even then, sometimes a lucky break was as critical as good detective work. She was sure they had the latter in this case, but they needed the former.

"I feel as if my life is on hold, waiting for the other shoe to drop," Donna said. "First the poisoned Stomach Soothers, then the bombing—what next? Why is someone out to destroy me and my family?"

"Right now, we don't have anything to show that the same person committed both crimes," Laura said. "It could be that the bombing was done to retaliate for the poisoned stomach medication."

"Who would do something like that?"

"People who are grieving sometimes react drastically," Laura said, thinking of Lydia Green's nephew and Jace's bruised face. "That doesn't at all excuse what was done, but it does give us motivation and an idea of where to look."

"You're thinking of Leo Elgin, aren't you?" Donna shook her head. "I've known Leo since he was a little boy. A smart, quiet boy. I can't imagine him killing someone—a wonderful woman like Lydia Green. Especially not when he's grieving his mother's death."

"We're looking at a lot of different people and motives," Laura said. "That was just one example."

The door to Donna's office opened and an attractive man with thick silver hair entered. He smiled at Laura. "I'm sorry, dear. I didn't mean to interrupt."

Donna half rose from her chair. "I didn't know you were coming in today."

"Oh, I thought I should come in and check on things." He moved into the room, then looked at Laura again. "It's good to see you. It's been a while, hasn't it?"

"Steve, this is—" Donna began.

"Oh, I know who it is." The man—Laura realized it must be Steve Stroud—waved away the interruption. "I'm not likely to forget our future daughter-in-law, am I?"

"Steve, this is Laura Lovejoy. She's Parker's new administrative assistant, not his fiancée." Donna's voice was firm. "Parker and Kathleen split up almost two years ago."

Steve's face clouded. "They did? I guess... I guess it just slipped my mind." He offered Laura a sheepish smile. "You do look a lot like her. A very pretty young woman." He turned back to his wife. "Is Parker here?"

"I don't know," Donna said. "He's been coming in late some mornings."

"That's all right." Steve's expression remained benign. "The boy works too hard. Always burning the midnight oil, working late."

Donna and Laura exchanged glances. Certainly since Laura had been here, Parker had not worked late. "Why don't you go into your office?" Donna suggested. "I'll send some reports in that I need you to review."

He looked relieved. "Of course I'll review them for you," he said. "I did always have more patience for that sort of thing than you do."

"Go on and I'll send them over in a minute," Donna said.

She waited until her husband had entered his office and shut the door behind him before she dropped into her chair once more. "I'm sorry about that," she said. "He's not supposed to drive, but sometimes he gets away from the caretaker I've hired and heads down here. I'll have to call the caretaker and find out what happened." She glanced toward the office door. "And as you can see, he's not always well-oriented to time and place. He mixes up the past and present and simply doesn't remember other things."

"Who was Kathleen?" Laura asked.

"A young woman Parker dated for a time. They were engaged for a little over six months. Then she broke off the relationship and moved away."

"Where is she now? Do you know?"

"The last I heard, she was living in Washington, DC."

"I'll need her full name and address so we can check." At Donna's astonished look, she added, "She probably had nothing to do with any of this, but we need to check out anyone who has had a relationship with the family." Maybe things between Parker and Kathleen hadn't been so amicable.

"All right," Donna said. "I'll get that information for you."

"All this must be very stressful for you," Laura said.

"It is. But there's nothing to do but carry on."

"Parker mentioned that he had tried to persuade you to let him take on more of the day-to-day operation of the business," Laura said.

"He has." Her expression hardened. "I know

that my son is not really your boss, at least not for the long term, but I still don't feel right discussing him with you this way."

"I'm only interested if it pertains to the case," Laura said. Not precisely true. She had a human curiosity to know more about the man she worked with every day. But she was professional enough not to give in to that curiosity.

"Then let's just say that I don't think Parker is ready for the responsibility of running this business," Donna said. "Especially not in this time of crisis." She stood again. "If you'll excuse me, I need to get some sort of paperwork to keep Steve occupied, before he decides to wander into the factory and cause trouble."

Laura left the office, pondering the dynamic between husband and wife. What would that be like, to watch the person you had vowed to love for better or worse slipping away right before your eyes?

When she reached her office, Laura was surprised to find Merry seated behind her desk. "Can I help you?" Laura asked, moving past the woman to stow her purse in the filing cabinet.

"I'm just waiting for Parker to come in." Merry swiveled back and forth in Laura's chair. "You're late."

"I stopped to talk with Mrs. Stroud."

"What would she want with you?"

Laura didn't bother answering the question.

"I'll tell Parker you stopped by when he gets in," she said. "Right now, I have work I need to do."

Merry made no move to leave, swiveling back and forth in the chair, a smirk on her face. "I think I'll wait here for Parker to get in."

"I don't care what you do, but you need to get out of my chair." Laura glared at the woman. She wasn't above yanking Merry out of the chair by her ponytail, but she hoped they could resolve this in a more adult fashion.

"I like this chair," Merry said. "It's more comfortable than mine."

Laura was debating her next move when the door behind them opened and Parker came in. "Good morning, Parker!" Merry called.

Parker looked from Laura to Merry. "What are you doing here?" he asked.

Merry vacated the chair at last and hurried around the desk. "I stopped by to say good morning," she said.

"Good morning," he said, then disappeared into his office and shut the door.

Merry stared at the closed door, looking close to tears. Laura settled into the chair behind her desk and booted up her computer.

"He doesn't like you," Merry said.

Laura looked up and Merry stalked over to the desk. "Parker was never like this when Cheryl worked for him. Having to work with you has put him in a bad mood."

Laura shrugged. "If you say so."

Merry leaned over the desk, both hands planted on its surface. "What are you doing here, anyway?"

"I'm trying to work." Laura turned back to her computer.

"Everyone thinks it's strange that you and your husband showed up here out of nowhere and the next day that bomb goes off. You're not even from here and you move into one of the top jobs at the company. We all think you're up to something."

"I'm not up to anything," Laura said.

"I think you are," Merry said. "And I'm going to find out what it is." She whirled and hurried away, reminding Laura of a defiant child. Her last words might as well have been, *I'm telling!*

"THE WARRANT CAME through to allow us to bug Leo Elgin's house," Jace said after dinner that evening. Laura had made tacos, so he was supposed to be cleaning up, though he lingered at the table over a glass of iced tea. His bruises looked worse than ever, though she had to admit the rugged look added an air of danger that suited him. "We'll go in tomorrow, during his mom's memorial service."

"What's your plan?" she asked. Jace always had a plan for these things. His aptitude for legal breaking and entering was one of the reasons he had been recruited for the tactical crime division.

"We're going in as caterers for the reception after the service."

"Leo is paying caterers for a reception?" He hadn't struck Laura as someone who would go to that much trouble.

"Stroud Pharmaceuticals arranged it all," he said. "Donna Stroud insisted."

"Ah." Laura nodded. "And we insisted that Donna Stroud insist."

"Ramirez might have encouraged her a little, but she doesn't know that we're going in or what we'll be doing."

"Of course not." She sighed. "What do you need me to do?"

He studied her across the table. "You need to get a wig," he said. "Something mousy. And a maid's uniform."

"I hope this isn't going where I think it's going," she said.

"Get your mind out of the gutter, Smitty," he said. "I'm not talking about a *French* maid. Frankly, we need to drab you down so you're less noticeable."

"Since when am I noticeable?" She stared at him. "I'm a federal agent. I know how to blend in."

"You know how to blend in when you're wearing your black suit with your hair in a bun. But here in Mayville—trust me, you stand out."

"What do you mean, I stand out?"

He grinned. "Do you know how many men have come up to me and said something about the hot new blonde in Parker's office?"

She flushed. "What did you say?"

"I told them, yeah, that's my wife, so hands off."

Her expression must have conveyed her annoyance. "Hey, it's what they expect," he said. "Don't take it personally."

How could she not take it personally? On one hand, it bothered her to know men at the plant had been talking about her. On the other hand, she melted a little at the thought of Jace warning them off—as if he really did care.

"Headquarters is sending over a package tomorrow morning," he said. "It should have everything we need, including the disguises I asked for."

"Good. Because I think if I go shopping for a wig in Mayville, it's going to spark rumors."

His grin was positively wicked. "Then you could tell them you were just trying to liven things up in the bedroom."

She threw her spoon at him, but he caught it in the air and laughed. "What's your disguise?" she asked.

"Glasses, earring and fake tattoos."

She frowned. "Someone could recognize you."

"Trust me, they won't."

She slept fitfully that night, anxiety over the

next day's job mingling with wild dreams of Jace—Jace kissing her, touching her, then leaving her, guaranteeing she awoke tired and out of sorts.

The promised box from headquarters arrived at nine thirty. The memorial service for Gini Elgin was due to begin at eleven. Jace figured they would have about an hour to get in and out before the real caterers showed up, followed by Leo and the other mourners. They each retired to their rooms to get ready.

The black pants, white shirt and gray apron were definitely on the drab side, Laura decided as she studied what she could see of herself in the dresser mirror. The wig—a mousy brown bob with thick bangs—also did little to draw attention to herself. She added the white Keds that had also been in the box, secured her weapon in its harness beneath the apron, and called it good.

She met up with Jace in the kitchen, where he was examining the electronics that had also been packed in their box. Laura stared at his transformation. He wore black pants and a tight black T-shirt that clung to his biceps and abs, showing off details she hadn't noticed before—mainly, that Jace Cantrell had put in his share of time in the gym. Below the short sleeves of the tee he'd added full-sleeve tattoos—a vividly colored tapestry of birds, fish, serpents and at least one skull.

A gold hoop glinted at one ear, and he'd shaved his scruff into a soul patch.

"Is this your idea of drabbing down and not standing out?" she asked, trying—and failing—to tear her eyes away from him.

"I'm going for the opposite effect," he said. "If anyone does see me, they'll remember the body art. Once we're done with the job, I'll remove the sleeves and the earring, shave off the soul patch and essentially, vanish."

At ten forty-five, they left the trailer. At a warehouse on the other end of town they traded the pickup for a panel van, Bread and Butter Caterers stenciled on the side. Jace drove past the church where Gini's service was being held. The parking lot was full and more parked cars lined either side of the street. From there, it was only five blocks to Gini's house, where Leo was staying. The cottage sat well back from the road in a grove of mature trees. Roses climbed trellises on either side of the front door, their scent heavy in the humid air.

They headed for the front door, carrying two plastic totes that to any passerby would look like supplies for the catered reception. Laura blocked the view from the road while Jace made quick work of the front door lock, which didn't even have a dead bolt. Then they were in.

Gini Elgin had favored hominess over haute couture in her furnishings, a sagging sofa with faded floral cushions sharing space in the living room with a scuffed maple coffee table, an armchair upholstered in gold velvet, and a braided rug in shades of brown and gold. Dust filmed every flat surface, and Laura wondered if Leo had even been in here since his return.

The dining room and a small home office had the same air of disuse and abandonment. Only the kitchen looked lived-in, with a stained coffee cup in the sink and an open box of cereal on the counter. Jace went to the brick-like cordless phone in its charging station on one end of the counter. "I'll start here," he said. "Set out the food, and then see if you can find his bedroom."

Laura unpacked a tray of finger sandwiches and another of cookies and set them on the kitchen island. The real caterers would bring more food later. She and Jace had carried these two trays as part of their cover.

She turned her attention to the search for Leo's bedroom. Though she knew the house was empty, she moved cautiously down the hall, as wary of leaving evidence behind as of surprising an unforeseen occupant of the house. The first door she reached led to a bathroom with avocado-green tiles and an old-fashioned claw-foot tub. A blue bath towel hung crookedly on the towel bar by the tub, and a man's shaving kit balanced on the edge of the sink.

Leo's bedroom was next door—a child's room

with a single unmade bed draped in a blue corduroy spread, posters for decades-old baseball players on the walls. Old athletic trophies shared space on a bookshelf with paperback thrillers and computer software manuals. A small desk in the corner held a laptop computer and a phone charger, minus the phone. Dirty dishes and fast food wrappers crowded the nightstand.

"This his room?" Jace looked in the doorway.

"Yeah." Laura stepped aside to let him get to the desk. "Pretty depressing. I think he's probably been spending most of his time in here."

"Makes our job easier." Jace assessed the room, then picked up the bedside lamp and examined it. "I'll put one bug here, another on the desk," he said. "It's overkill, but we've got the hardware, so why not use it?"

While he worked, Laura searched the bookcase, closet and dresser drawers. She felt under the mattress, looked behind the curtains and shone a flashlight into the heating vents, looking for any secret stash. The local police had already searched the house once and hadn't found anything linking Leo to the explosion at Stroud Pharmaceuticals, but it never hurt to give everything a second going-over.

"If he did plant that bomb, I think he made the device somewhere else," Jace said.

"Where else?" Laura asked. "This place doesn't even have a garage, just that little shed out back, and the report from the search team says it's full of gardening tools."

"A storage unit, maybe. An abandoned barn? There are probably a few of those around here."

"Maybe we'll hear something that will give us a better idea." She watched him fit the tiny listening device into the base of a stapler that sat on one corner of the desk, then snap the bottom of the stapler back in place.

She hugged her arms across her chest. "Let's get out of here," she said. "This place gives me the creeps."

He stowed his tools and they headed toward the door. One step into the hallway, Jace froze.

"What's wrong? Why did you stop?" She shoved at his back, then went cold all over as she recognized the sound of the front door opening, and someone coming inside.

Chapter Eight

Laura's anxiety radiated around her and through Jace. He reached back, grabbed her hand and squeezed.

"I'm okay," she whispered.

He released her hand and moved forward, stopping at the end of the hallway as Leo rounded the corner toward them. The younger man, face pale and eyes reddened, stared at them. "Who are you?" he demanded, his voice shaky.

"We're from the caterer." Jace extended a hand and Leo automatically took it. "We weren't expecting anyone so soon."

Leo dropped Jace's hand, and his gaze shifted away. "I... I needed to get out of there," he said.

"We're very sorry for your loss." Laura adopted a Southern accent and prayed Leo wouldn't see past her disguise to the woman who had chatted him up at the bar last night.

"What were you doing back there?" Leo looked past them, toward the back of the house.

"We like to check that the bathroom is ready for guests," Laura said.

Leo scowled. "It took two of you to do that?"

She didn't miss a beat. "There was a spider in the sink. I asked Jeff to kill it for me."

Great improvisation, Jace thought, though Laura didn't strike him as the type to freak out over a spider. In fact, the only time he'd ever seen her lose her cool was when he kissed her. She'd all but melted in his arms, making him believe that even if she resisted the idea of getting involved with him, she wanted him.

Now was not the time to be thinking about that, he reminded himself.

"You need to leave," Leo said.

"We won't be much longer," Jace said. "We just need to arrange a few things."

"No! I don't want you here." Leo's voice rose, his eyes wild. "It's bad enough I have to put up with all these people coming over after the funeral. You can at least leave me alone for now."

"All right." Laura took Jace's arm. "We can finish later."

They moved past him toward the kitchen, but paused in the hallway to listen as he made his way down the hall and shut the door to his room behind him. "Let's go," Laura said.

They left the food, grabbed up both totes and headed out the front door. Jace started the van, drove around the corner and parked behind a deserted office complex.

He texted Rogers that they werc out, then leaned his head back against the seat and let out a breath, waiting for his racing heart to slow. As operations went, he had been in tighter spots. Still, it was unnerving when the surveillance subject found you in his house.

"Why did he leave his own mother's funeral scarcely twenty minutes into the service?" Laura asked.

"Funerals are hard for a lot of people," Jace said. "Maybe it got to him and he just wanted to be alone."

"Maybe." She swiveled toward him. "Drive back around to where we can get a good look at the house."

"All right." He started the engine again and drove around the block, parking at the end of the street, where they had a clear view of Leo's driveway and front door. They had scarcely parked when a white Chevy sedan turned onto the street.

Laura gasped as the sedan passed, the driver never even glancing in their direction. "That's Merry Winger," she said.

"Remind me who she is."

"She's Parker Stroud's girlfriend."

Merry turned into the Elgins' driveway, got out and walked up to the door. She was a pretty blonde in a neat navy-blue miniskirt and a sleeveless white blouse, and very tall white heels. She rang the bell and a moment later, Leo answered the door.

"He doesn't look happy to see her," Laura said. She had pulled a pair of binoculars from the backpack at her feet and was studying the couple. As she said this, Leo stepped aside to let Merry in, and shut the door behind her.

Laura lowered the glasses. "How did you know he was going to meet someone?" Jace asked.

"It was just a hunch." She continued to stare toward the door. "But what is Parker's girlfriend doing meeting Leo Elgin in secret?"

"We don't know that it's secret."

"He left his mother's funeral to meet up with her. That's pretty secretive, if you ask me." She leaned forward, as if that would help her see through the closed door. "And where is Parker?"

"Maybe Leo and Merry have a thing on the side?" Jace speculated. "Or they were a couple before and now that he's back in town she's trying to renew the acquaintance?"

The door opened and Merry emerged. Head down, she hurried to her car, then drove away. Laura sat back in her seat. "She wasn't in there long enough to do anything," she said.

"He didn't even walk her to the door," Jace said. "So maybe they're not having an affair. Or maybe she came on to him and he turned her down."

Laura stowed the binoculars again. "Let's head back to the trailer. Maybe your recording devices will pick up something useful."

"HE HASN'T HAD a single phone call in the last twenty-four hours," Rogers said when Jace checked in with him Sunday afternoon. "No visitors since the reception after the funeral, and all of those conversations are variations of either condolences over the loss of his mother, or questions about what he plans to do next."

"What does he plan to do next?" Jace asked.

"He doesn't know. That's the answer he gave everyone, and if they tried to press, he either changed the subject or clammed up entirely."

"What about Merry Winger—the woman who showed up right after Laura and I left? What did they talk about?"

"She delivered something," Rogers said. "Here. Let me play you the recording."

Sound of door opening.
Leo: What do you want?
Merry: I brought you this.
Leo: You'd better go.
Merry: Not until you tell me what's going on.
Leo: Unintelligible mumble.
Merry: No. You men are all alike. You think I'm stupid and I'm not.
Leo: You need to go now.

Long pause. High heels clicking on hardwood. Slamming door.

"Any idea what she brought him?" Jace asked.

"It could have been a sympathy card or a cake or plastic explosives," Rogers said. "We can't tell from his reaction."

"Merry works in the Stroud offices with Laura. Let's see what she can find out. In the meantime, we need eyes on Leo."

"We don't have enough people to babysit him full time," Rogers said. "At this point we don't have any proof he's even worth watching. It was a stretch getting the okay to bug his place."

"I'll watch him after my shift at the factory," Jace said.

"When will you sleep?"

"When he does. You can keep an eye on him while I'm at the factory."

"I have other work to do," Rogers said.

"When you have a free moment," Jace said. "Just for a few days."

Rogers grunted, which Jace chose to take as agreement. "What do you think we're going to find out?" Rogers asked.

"Who he's seeing, where he's going. If he assembled that explosive, he did it somewhere other than his mother's house."

"I'm willing to try for a few days," Rogers

said. "But I'm not convinced we're not wasting our time."

Jace ended the call and looked up to find Laura studying him. "You're going to surveil Leo?" she asked.

"Merry brought him something yesterday. From the tone of their conversation, I don't think she was the person he was expecting to see, and he got rid of her as fast as he could."

"What did she bring him?"

"We don't know. The bugs haven't picked up any other suspicious conversations."

"So, if he left the funeral to meet someone, they either didn't show, or they sent Merry instead," Laura said.

"That's what I'm thinking."

"Maybe Parker sent her." The frown lines on Laura's forehead deepened. "I got the impression if he said jump, she'd ask, how high?"

"Talk to her. See what you can find out."

"I'll try, but I'm not her favorite person. Apparently, she applied to be Parker's admin before I stepped in and took the job."

"Yeah, but it sounds to me like she wants to keep an eye on Parker. Maybe you can offer to be her spy."

Laura stared at him. "You really think she wants to keep tabs on him? I thought she wanted to be closer to him."

He shrugged. "Hey, I never claimed to be an

expert on relationships. But I'm betting Parker wouldn't have picked her for the job. Most men don't like the woman they're involved with always looking over their shoulder."

He couldn't begin to decipher the look she shot him, though he would describe it as somewhere between disgust and incredulity. He started to reassure her that he knew she wasn't the type to get all up in his business, but bit back the words. He and Laura weren't "involved." Never mind that he couldn't be in the same room with her without being hyperaware of her: of her soft scent, her softer skin, and the hard shell around her emotions that he ached to break through.

"I'll see what I can do," she said. "What's your next move?"

He grabbed a backpack with binoculars, camera, water and snacks off the floor beside his chair. "I'm going to keep an eye on Leo. Don't wait up."

The first thing Laura noticed when she arrived at Stroud Pharmaceuticals on Monday was that the damage to the side door to the executive offices had been repaired, the police tape removed, and the sidewalk replaced, and everything sported a new coat of paint. A crew must have worked all weekend to effect the transformation.

Once inside, however, she noted people still avoided the area. Whether out of superstition or real fear, she couldn't tell. Her coworkers' reactions to her were still subdued, but she pretended not to notice. Maybe in their shoes, she'd be suspicious of the new couple, too. She didn't need to be best friends with any of these people in order to do her job.

She detoured to the break room and fetched two cups of coffee and two doughnuts from the open box on the table, then headed for Merry's desk. The younger woman looked up as Laura approached, eyes narrowed. "What do you want?" she asked.

"I need your advice." Laura set a cup of coffee and a doughnut in front of Merry, then slid a chair close to her desk.

Merry clearly hadn't expected this. "What kind of advice?" she asked, still wary.

"I want to do a good job," Laura said. "But Mr. Stroud—Parker—doesn't seem very happy with my performance. I figure you're the person who knows him best, so I thought maybe you could give me some tips on how to get on his good side."

"Why should I help you do the job I wanted?" Merry asked. "The job I still want?"

"I thought maybe I could do you a favor, too." Laura focused on stirring a packet of sugar into her coffee. "I know you and Parker have to be discreet about your relationship, what with working together and everything. I can make it easier for you to get in to see him, and I can make sure you have all the access you want."

"I can see Parker anytime." Merry tossed her head. "I don't need your help."

"I can run interference if anyone tries to interrupt you," Laura said. "And I can give you his schedule so you know when he's free."

"Why would you want to help me?" Merry asked.

"Because I need your help to do my job," Laura said. "And because Parker is always in a better mood after he's talked to you." The last part was a blatant lie, but she was counting on Merry wanting to believe it.

Merry relaxed a little. "I can give you a few pointers for dealing with him," she said. "But I can't promise they'll help. It could be he just doesn't like you." Her smirk said clearly that she didn't blame Parker.

"I'm grateful for any advice you can give me," Laura said, keeping her face straight.

Merry took a bite of doughnut and chewed, looking thoughtful. "I can't believe I'm even suggesting this to you, of all people," she said after she had swallowed. "But Parker likes women who keep themselves up. He'd probably like it if you dressed a little sexier—you know, shorter skirts and lower necklines."

Fat chance of that happening, but Laura nodded, her expression neutral. "Anything else?"

"He likes it when I compliment him. You know, some men need women to build up their egos."

Did she really believe that? "But you're his girlfriend," Laura said. "I'm just his assistant."

"Well, yeah." Merry shrugged. "I don't know what to tell you. Maybe smile more or have a better attitude. If he's grumpy around you, you must be doing something wrong."

Or maybe he's just a jerk, Laura thought. "I'll keep that in mind." She stood. "Thanks."

"Just remember—you owe me."

"I'll remember." She started to turn away, but hesitated. "Hey, did you go to Gini Elgin's services Saturday?" she asked.

"Yes. Why do you care?"

"I just wondered. I drove by the church and it looked like there were a lot of people there."

"Yeah, there was a big crowd."

"I guess you went with Parker, huh?"

"Well, yeah, though we had to pretend we weren't together when his parents were around." Merry rolled her eyes. "It's so silly, but Parker says I just have to be patient. All this fuss about the poisoned medication and the bomb is slowing everything down."

"I'm sure your patience will pay off," Laura said. "How was Gini's son—Leo?"

Confusion clouded Merry's eyes. "How do you know Leo?"

"I met him in town. He seemed really torn up about his mom's death."

"Yeah. They were close."

"Do you know him well?" Laura asked.

Merry wrinkled her nose. "No."

"I thought somebody told me the two of you used to date."

Merry laughed. "Me and Leo? Get out of here! Somebody was pulling your leg. He's definitely not my type." She shook her head, emphatic.

"I guess I misheard." Laura stepped away. "I'd better get to work. I'll talk to you later." She headed to her office, reviewing the conversation with Merry. She didn't think Merry was lying about her relationship with Leo. Gini's son wasn't handsome, wealthy, powerful or charming—all things Merry appeared to value. If she wasn't in a relationship with him, she must have gone to see him on Parker's behalf.

Parker was already in the office when Laura arrived. He turned from her desk. "Where have you been?" he demanded.

Laura moved around the desk and slid into her chair. "I was talking to Merry."

"About what?"

"About you." She looked him in the eye. One of her early trainers had stressed the importance of sticking to the truth whenever possible. "I was asking her how I could do a better job for you."

"As if Merry would know anything about that," he scoffed.

"She's your girlfriend, isn't she?"

He frowned. "I guess she told you that."

"Yes. Why? Is it a big secret?"

"It isn't appropriate for me to be dating an employee of the company." He tapped his index finger on the papers in her in-box. "So don't mention it to anyone."

"Your secret is safe with me." She smiled and he took a step back. Before he could escape to his office, she asked, "How was the service for Gini Elgin? I drove by there Saturday and it looked like a big crowd."

"Gini had a lot of friends," Parker said. "She'll be missed."

"How's your friend Leo?"

"I don't imagine he's doing very well, considering his mother was killed."

"Do the police have any suspects yet?" she asked.

"I don't think so. We'll probably never know who did something so horrible." He turned away. "Block off the rest of my morning. I have a meeting with my mother." Not waiting for an answer, he left the office.

She settled behind her desk. She hadn't learned anything new from her questioning of Merry and Parker. Not that she had expected them to spill their secrets to the nosy new employee, but the lack of progress in the case frustrated her.

The door opened and Merry sauntered in. "I want to see Parker," she said, and headed for his office.

"He's not here," Laura said. "He said he had a meeting with his mother."

Merry pouted. "He really ought to be in charge of this place, not her." She sank into the chair across from Laura's desk. "Honestly, she treats him like a child. When we're married, things are going to be different. I'm not going to let her run over him this way."

Laura opened her mouth to ask what Merry intended to say to Mrs. Stroud when the building shuddered, and a deafening roar surrounded them. Both women dropped to their knees on the floor as pictures, coffee cups and a vase of flowers slid to the floor and shattered. As the concussion subsided, screams rose to take its place. Laura was on her feet and running, Merry at her heels.

"What happened?" The younger woman screamed as people, some bleeding, others showered with debris, raced past them, out of the building.

Laura shoved her way through the crowd, toward the source of the commotion. "I think there was another bomb," she said, more to herself than to Merry. Why had she been too late to stop it?

Chapter Nine

The man and woman looked up when Ana tapped on the partially open door to the hospital room. "Mrs. Stroud? We need to ask you and your son some questions."

Donna Stroud, her face washed of color except for the purple half moons beneath her eyes, pressed her lips together tightly and nodded. Parker, on his back in the hospital bed, white bandaging swathing his forehead, said nothing, though his gaze bored into Ana and Rogers as they entered the small room, which smelled of antiseptic and dry-erase marker. "How are you feeling, Mr. Stroud?" Ana asked.

"About like I would expect a person to feel who's been blown up." He pressed a button by his side to raise the head of the bed. "They tell me I have a concussion and contusions, which is medical talk for being beaten half to death."

"Where were you when the blast occurred?" Rogers asked.

"I was standing just outside the door to my mother's office. I was about to go in."

"Did you know Ms. Dupree was in the office?" Rogers asked.

"No. I didn't know anyone was in there."

"This is so horrible." Donna spoke in a hoarse voice, just above a whisper. "Angela wasn't just an employee. She was a friend." She swallowed hard. "I can't believe she's gone."

"Do you know why Ms. Dupree was in your office yesterday morning?" Ana asked.

Donna shook her head. "I don't know. But it wouldn't have been unusual for her to stop by and say hello. We often chatted at work."

"Ms. Dupree's assistant, Shania Merritt, said her boss was bringing some pay raise authorizations for you to okay," Ana said.

Donna nodded. "That sounds right."

"Why weren't you in the office, Mrs. Stroud?" Rogers asked. "Wouldn't you usually be there at that time of morning?"

"Yes, but…" She glanced at Parker. "My husband isn't well."

"Is this to do with his dementia, or something else?" Ana asked.

Donna looked pained. "Steve is forgetful, although most days he manages fine. But sometimes, he's frustrated by his inability to remember and gets confused. Then he becomes angry and we argue. Yesterday morning he was especially combative and I stayed home to try to calm him down."

"What was he being combative about?" Ana asked.

"He had gotten it into his head that Parker was negotiating to sell the business to a competitor and he insisted we should fire Parker." She shook her head. "It's utter nonsense, of course, but once he gets an idea like this into his head, there's no reasoning with him."

"Where would he get such an idea?" Rogers asked.

"There's no basis in reality for these delusions," Parker said. "It's a symptom of his disease. He could see something on TV or dream something and believe it's real."

"What were you doing outside your mother's office, Mr. Stroud?" Rogers asked. "Wouldn't you normally be in your own office at that time?"

"I wanted to speak to my mother about the production schedule for next month. As the factory manager, I often consult with her."

"Your assistant, Ms. Lovejoy, told us you told her you had a meeting scheduled with your mother," Ana said. "She was told to leave your calendar clear for the whole morning because of this meeting."

"Yes, that's right."

Ana turned to Donna. "We didn't see any notice on your calendar of such a meeting, Mrs. Stroud."

"My son doesn't have to make an appointment to consult with me."

"So this wasn't a prescheduled meeting?" Rogers asked.

"No," Parker said. "If Ms. Lovejoy thought that, she was mistaken."

Or perhaps Parker had wanted Laura to think the meeting had been scheduled earlier, for whatever reason. Ana turned her attention to Donna again. The woman seemed to have aged five years since their first meeting a week ago. "I know you've answered this question before, but we need to ask again," she said. "Can you think of anyone who might wish to harm you?"

"Are you suggesting my mother was the target for this madman?" Parker asked.

"The bomb was in her office, we think under her desk," Rogers said. "It was designed to trigger when she opened her bottom desk drawer." He looked to Donna, who had blanched even paler. "We were told that drawer is where you keep a box of tissues and some other personal items."

She nodded. "I don't know of anyone who would…" She wet her lips. "Who would want to kill me?"

Parker struggled to sit up in bed. "You're upsetting my mother. Don't you think she's been through enough?"

"Why would Angela open that drawer?" Ana asked. "Do you know?"

"I... I can guess."

They waited as Donna stared at her fingers laced together in her lap. When she looked up, her eyes were desolate. "Angela was recently diagnosed with breast cancer. She was due to have surgery, then chemotherapy the week after. I was the only person she told. We had cried together over the news. I can guess that if she came to talk to me yesterday, she was going to let me know her treatment schedule. We would have cried again. When she didn't find me there, maybe she got teary-eyed. She knew I kept tissues in that drawer, so she might have opened it, intending to pull herself together before she went back into the outer office."

"Did you see anyone suspicious in or around the office that day or the day before?" Rogers asked Parker.

"No."

"Mrs. Stroud? Did you see anything or anyone suspicious?"

Donna shook her head. "No."

"Have you received any threatening letters or phone calls?" Ana asked.

"Only the one letter I gave you—the 'six for six' message. Nothing else."

"Are you going to find the person who did this?" Parker asked. "Because you're not doing a very good job so far."

Ana ignored the dig. In his place, she would

probably have been frustrated by the lack of progress in the case, too. Civilians expected law enforcement to solve crimes quickly, in the space of a few days. Building a case and finding the guilty party usually took much longer. "Have you considered closing the plant temporarily?" she asked Donna.

"Out of the question," Parker said.

Donna's answer was less strident. "We have a hundred employees and their families who depend on us," she said. "We can't shut them out. As it is, we had to temporarily lay off fifty people when we shut down the plant that made the Stomach Soothers."

"We need you to find whoever is doing this so we can put this tragedy behind us," Parker said.

"This case is our top priority," Rogers said. A nurse entered the room and he moved toward the door. "We may need to talk to you again."

He and Ana moved into the hallway. He waited until they had reached their rental car before he spoke. "What do you think?"

"I think someone has targeted these people," she said.

"Leo Elgin?"

"Maybe. Has your surveillance turned up anything on him?" He and Jace had been trading off watching Leo during daylight hours.

"No. The plant is closed today, so Jace is

watching Elgin. If he doesn't turn up anything, we need to focus on someone else."

"Who?"

"We're going to look at everyone who had access to that office," Rogers said.

"Donna Stroud had access," Ana said. "And she was conveniently not there this morning."

"Do you think she killed two of her employees and sabotaged her own product?"

"I think we both know criminals who have done stranger things."

He nodded. "Let's look closer at her and see if we can find out."

"And let's talk to that competitor Steve Stroud accused Parker of negotiating with. Maybe someone is angling to get Stroud Pharmaceuticals at a bargain price."

"Good idea." One more item on the long list of threads to pull in this case. This was the tedious part of working a case—following leads that went nowhere, talking to people who might or might not have something to hide and trying to put all the information together to form a picture that led to the guilty party. It took hours of effort and focus, but that, more than bravery or cunning, was what solved most cases. It was one reason the bureau hired as many accountants as military types. Brains counted more than brawn more often than not.

FOUR TO GO.

Merry had placed the envelope on the top of the pile of mail Tuesday morning, and pointed it out to Donna when she delivered it. "It looks like the other letter, doesn't it?" she asked, leaning in close, so that Donna caught the scent of her perfume—floral and delicate, if applied with a heavy hand. "The one the FBI was so concerned about."

Donna stared at the plain white envelope, with her name in dark block letters, no title, and the address for Stroud Pharmaceuticals. "Aren't you going to open it?" Merry asked.

"I think I should call the police," Donna said. "Or maybe Agent Ramirez. I have her card in my desk somewhere." But she made no move to search for it, fixated on the envelope.

"What if it's a solicitation from the local funeral home or something?" Merry asked. "I mean, really?" She plucked the envelope from the stack of mail and slid one pink-polished nail beneath the flap.

"You'll destroy fingerprints," Donna protested.

Merry shook her head. "Every criminal knows to wear gloves." She flicked open the envelope flap and dumped the contents onto the desk. The half sheet of copy paper lay crookedly on the blotter, twenty-point type exclaiming, *Four to go!*

Donna gasped and swayed.

"Mrs. Stroud, you've gone all pale." Merry took her arm and eased her back in her chair.

"You sit there and take deep breaths. You've had a shock." She left, then returned with a cup of water from the cooler in the corner. "Drink this."

Donna drank and began to feel a little steadier. "Thank you." She glanced at the words on the paper and suppressed a shudder, then opened her desk drawer and took out Ana Ramirez's card. "I'd better telephone for someone to deal with this."

"What does that mean?" Merry asked. "'Four to go'?"

"I don't know," Donna lied. Though she knew very well what it meant. Six people had died from taking poisoned Stomach Soothers. Two people had perished in the two bombings at Stroud Pharmaceuticals. Four more deaths before the score would be even, in the bomber's twisted logic.

JACE WAS NUMB with boredom after three nights of tailing Leo Elgin, but he forced himself to stick with the surveillance. The man might be the dullest person Jace had ever met, but that didn't mean he wasn't up to no good.

Though, as far as Jace could tell from the bugs he'd placed in the house, Leo wasn't up to anything but sitting in front of his computer playing hundreds of rounds of solitaire. He received no visitors or phone calls, and the only person he attempted to call was Parker Stroud. The afternoon after the bomb exploded that killed Angela Dupree, Leo tried to call Parker, who was in the hospital, six times. Parker never answered, though that wasn't too surprising, given that he was injured. Leo left only one message. "This is Leo. What's going on over there?"

Jace slumped in a van with the logo of a fake pest control company, parked on the street with a clear view of Elgin's house. Times like these, he missed smoking the most, even though smoking while on surveillance was forbidden—the scent of smoke might attract attention. Still, he missed how smoking gave him something to do with his hands and something to focus on besides his own breathing.

Movement in the house, followed by the sound of a door opening and closing. Jace sat up straighter. It sounded as if Leo had left the house, but Jace saw no movement near the front door. Had Leo gone out the back? Jace got out of the van and, walking purposefully, he marched down the sidewalk. When he reached Leo's house, he ducked down the side, into a screen of shrubbery between Leo's house and the neighbor's. He reached the backyard in time to see Leo unlock the door to a wooden shed in the back corner. With a sagging roof and sides almost devoid of paint, the shed looked on the verge of collapse.

Jace shoved further into the screen of bushes, gritting his teeth as thorns raked his arms and face. He could hear movement from inside the shed—something heavy being shoved around. He headed toward the back of the little building, hoping for a window or a missing board that would allow him to see inside. But instead of an opening, he discovered the back of the shed was all but covered by a five-foot mound of dirt and sod, as if the shed had been built into the side of a hill.

But this was no hill. Jace had seen a similar structure at his grandparents' farm. At some point the Elgins, or whoever had owned the property before them, had built an old-fashioned root cellar. Rather than digging out a space underground, they had built up the earth around the shed. Somewhere inside there was probably a door leading into the storage area within the mound of dirt.

The FBI had searched the Elgin property, but would they have recognized the root cellar?

Jace retreated the way he had come, and walked back to his van. He called Rogers. "The people who searched the Elgin home. Did they look in the root cellar?" he asked.

"Let me check." A moment later Rogers was on the line again. "There's no mention of a root cellar."

"It's at the back of that old shed, built into a mound of earth," Jace said. "They need to check it."

"We're not going to get another warrant," Rogers said. "We've already had complaints that we're harassing the locals and not finding anything."

"There's something going on in that shed," Jace said. "Leo is in there now. I could hear him moving stuff around."

"Maybe he's finally clearing out his mother's property."

"He's been calling Parker Stroud, leaving cryptic messages. Something is going on."

"Find proof then. You haven't got enough to go on."

Jace ended the call and sat back. He'd find the proof. He punched in another number.

Laura answered on the second ring. "Hello?"

"Don't wait up. I'll be working all night."

"What is it? Have you found something?"

"Maybe."

"What is it?"

"I don't know yet, but I need to hang around here tonight. I'll talk to you later."

He started to hang up, but her voice stopped him. "Jace?"

"Yeah?"

"Be careful."

She ended the call. He sat with the phone in his hand, an unsettling tremor in his chest. It was the kind of thing anyone might say to another person. But Laura wasn't just any other person, and when she had told him to be careful, she had sounded as if she really cared.

LAURA TUCKED HER phone back into her pocket. Why had she said that to Jace—"be careful"—as if she were his mother or his wife or something? She should have been demanding he tell her what he was up to. After all, they were partners in this investigation.

She pulled out her phone and hit Redial. "Yeah?" Jace answered.

"What is going on?" she asked. "What are you doing?"

"You don't want to know."

She gripped the phone harder. "Tell me."

"I think Leo is up to something in the old garden shed behind his house—or rather, in the attached root cellar."

"And?" There had to be an *and*.

"I'm going to wait until after dark and sneak in there and look around."

"You don't have a warrant." If he had a warrant, he wouldn't have hesitated to tell her. "Not only is what you're proposing illegal, nothing you find could be used in evidence. You'll compromise the whole case." This was just like him, wanting to take shortcuts, thinking the rules didn't apply to him. He'd gotten away with this kind of thing before now because he had good results, but this time he was going too far.

"I'm not compromising the case." His voice was calm, as if they'd been discussing what to eat for dinner. "I know how to get in and out without leaving a trace, and I won't touch anything. I just want to see if my hunch is right. Then I'll be able to get a warrant."

"How will you get a warrant if you don't reveal what you find in there?" she asked.

"I'll say I saw Leo do something suspicious, or carrying a suspicious object." She swore she could almost *hear* his sly grin. "It won't take much. I can be very persuasive."

"But you'd be lying!" She didn't even try to keep the horror from her voice. "You'd be manufacturing evidence."

"I wouldn't be manufacturing anything. I'll only speak to what I will know is in that root cellar."

"It's still a lie."

"A very small one, and for a good cause."

That's probably what every corrupt agent or politician or businessperson said when they started. But little lies led to big ones. And big lies led to the corruption of the whole situation. "Jace, don't do this," she said, unable to keep the pleading from her voice.

"Why not?" he asked.

"Because you're better than this."

He was silent so long she thought he had hung up. "Jace?" she asked.

"I'm here." He blew out a breath. "I need to get in there and look around," he said. "If Leo is responsible for those bombs, he's killed two people already. We can't let him kill anyone else."

"No." She felt her convictions wavering. Was Jace right, that the ends—stopping a murderer—justified the means? But then, where did she draw the line? "You can't lie to get the warrant," she said.

"Let me go in and see what I find," he said. "Maybe I'm wrong and I'm wasting our time. At least then we'll know we need to focus on someone beside Leo."

"All right."

"Right. Gotta go."

"Jace?"

"What?"

"Be careful."

THE ELGIN HOUSE was located in an older neighborhood on the edge of town. Most of the houses looked to have been built in the seventies or eighties and were occupied by older couples. By midnight, every house on the block was silent and dark. Leo had turned off the last light in his place an hour before and hadn't moved since.

Jace, dressed in jeans and a black hoodie, slipped out of the van and made his way along the side of the yard to the back, not in the bushes this time, but alongside them, concealed by deepest shadow. The night air was still and humid, like furnace exhaust, without a hint of coolness.

Within five minutes, he was sweating in the heavy sweatshirt.

The shed and root cellar hunched in the back corner of the yard, looking even more decrepit in the washed-out light of a quarter moon. Jace checked the windows on that side of the house for any sign of movement, but found none. Heart pounding, he stepped into the moonlight and walked over to the door.

Using his body as a shield, he trained the beam of a small penlight on the lock, a hefty padlock, so shiny it couldn't have been on here long. The lock was threaded through a rusty hasp—but the hasp was fashioned with new screws. *What are you so concerned about locking up in here, Leo?* Jace wondered. He'd have to check the records to see if this lock had been here when the FBI conducted their warranted search.

He studied the lock a moment, then took out a set of picks and went to work. The standard commercial lock popped open in less than two minutes. Jace lifted the hasp, opened the door, then hung the lock in place and slipped inside.

The shed smelled of mildew and weed killer. The penlight revealed a shovel, rake and hoe on nails along the far wall. Bags of potting soil and several five-gallon buckets crammed with wood scraps and bits of rusty metal crowded the floor. A leaning metal shelf against the side wall held flower pots, bags of fertilizer and enough weed killing concoctions to poison half the town. If one of them had been found in the Stomach Soothers, Jace would have been suspicious Leo had decided to take out his own mother.

The root cellar was on the other side of the back wall. Jace played his light over the rough wood siding, looking for any kind of opening. It couldn't be obvious or the previous searchers would have found it right away. They would have found most hidden doors as well, so this had to be something especially clever.

A big copper pot, the kind once used for boiling clothing over an outside fire, took up most of the back corner of the shed, filled with tangled fishing gear and an old tarp. Recalling the noises he had heard when Leo first entered the shed, of something heavy being moved, Jace dragged the pot out of the way and shone his light into the corner.

Nothing looked out of the ordinary. The weathered boards of the shed appeared firmly nailed in place. One rusting nail stuck out of the wood a scant quarter inch. When Jace tugged at the nail, it didn't move. But when he grasped the nail like a handle and attempted to pull it, the whole section of siding slid toward him, and a wave of cooler air washed over him, smelling of machine oil and damp.

He stilled, ears straining for any sound, but all remained silent. He stepped around the pot and ducked into the opening. The root cellar was not large, perhaps five feet deep and seven feet wide, like a large closet, the ceiling so low he had to hunch to keep from brushing the top of his head against the chicken wire that had been used as a frame to support the sod laid over it. A wooden work bench took up most of the space, with a small drill press, scales, and various hand tools littering its top. Cardboard apple boxes filled the space beneath the bench. Jace nudged the lid off one box and let out a soft whistle as he played his light across the collection of wire, fuses, blasting caps, and a hefty bundle of dynamite.

The other boxes contained metal pipes, and some electronics he thought must be part of timing mechanisms. If the bomb-making materials matched those used in the Stroud explosions, there was enough evidence here to put Leo away for a very long time. He switched off the light and backed out of the root cellar. He had just shoved the copper pot back into place and was moving toward the door when the clank of the padlock against the hasp and a soft curse made his heart stop beating.

He had just enough time to dive into the front corner and pull a tarp over his head before the door opened and Leo stepped inside.

Chapter Ten

Jace couldn't see through the tarp, which smelled of mud and decay. He crouched beneath it, one hand on the gun at his hip, his body tensed to spring if Leo discovered his hiding place. But Leo's footsteps moved away, toward the back corner. The copper pot scraped across the floor, a faint sliding sound announced the opening of the secret door, and something rattled on or beneath the workbench.

Jace risked rearranging the tarp so that he could peer from beneath it. Leo had switched on a light—maybe a battery-operated lantern—inside the root cellar, and its yellow glow illuminated the back of the shed as well. Jace had a limited view of a space just to the right of the secret door. He could hear Leo moving around in there, jostling boxes, rearranging tools. Unable to sleep, had he decided to build another bomb?

Seconds later, Leo emerged from the root cellar, carrying one of the apple boxes. He exited the shed, footsteps retreating across the yard.

Jace's ears rang in the silence that followed. He remained still, counting to one hundred, giving Leo time to return to the house. He waited for the sound of the door opening and closing, but it didn't come. Instead, just as he was debating throwing off the tarp and making his way back to his van, a car started somewhere very nearby. Was Leo leaving the house, taking the apple box somewhere?

But instead of growing fainter as Leo drove away, the roar of the car's engine grew louder, until the vehicle was idling right outside the shed door. Then the engine died, the car door slammed, and Leo was inside the shed once more. He retrieved a second box from the root cellar, carried it to the car, then returned a third time.

Jace shifted beneath the tarp. He couldn't risk leaving his hiding place. But he couldn't let Leo move his bomb-making operation out of the shed without trying to stop him. He eased his phone from his pocket and tapped out a text to Laura: SOS I NEED YOU HERE ASAP.

ADRENALINE SURGED THROUGH Laura as she read Jace's text. She traded the shorts she was wearing for jeans, pulled on her weapon harness and boots, and grabbed a big flashlight that could double as a truncheon. In the truck, she called Ramirez. Though she had probably been asleep at this late hour, Ana sounded alert. "What's going on?" she asked.

"I just got a text from Jace," Laura said. "He's at Leo's place and it sounds like he's in trouble."

"What was he doing at Leo's at this hour?"

"He said something about a shed in the backyard. He'd seen suspicious activity around it." She didn't want to get Jace in trouble with the complete truth, and she didn't want to jeopardize their case.

"We'll be right there," Ramirez said.

Laura pushed the truck hard across town through the darkened streets, mind racing. Jace had planned to search the shed behind Leo's house. Had Leo surprised him? Had Leo shot him? Pain squeezed her chest at the thought, and she pressed harder on the gas, hands whiteknuckled on the steering wheel.

She turned onto Leo's street and spotted Jace's van right away. She parked behind it, then ran to Leo's house. She drew her weapon and, keeping to the darkest shadows, she headed for the backyard, where Jace had said the shed was located.

She spotted the car first, the driver's door and the trunk open, spilling light onto the weedy space in front of a leaning wooden shed. She froze as someone emerged from the shed. Leo, carrying a cardboard box.

A car passed in front of the house. Leo didn't even look up. He stowed the box in the trunk of the car and returned to the shed. Her phone vibrated and she pulled it from her pocket and glanced at the screen. Where are you? From Ramirez.

North side of the property, toward the back. Leo is at the shed.

Moments later, two dark shapes moved toward her. She waited until they were almost on her before she whispered, "Over here."

Ramirez moved in close behind her, followed by Rogers. "What's going on?" Ramirez asked.

"Leo's moving something out of that shed."

"Any sign of Jace?"

Laura shook her head. She could try to text him, but what if he wasn't in a position to answer her?

Leo emerged from the shed again with another box. "What's he got?" Rogers asked.

"I think we should find out," Laura said. She pulled the big Maglite from her belt, aimed it toward Leo and pressed the on switch.

"FBI!" Rogers shouted. "Drop the box and put your hands in the air."

Leo dropped the box and looked around wildly. "Put your hands up!" Rogers ordered, his voice booming.

Leo tentatively stretched his hands up. Ramirez and Rogers raced forward. Laura hung back, keeping the light trained on Leo and her face in the shadows. If possible, she and Jace needed to protect their cover.

While Ramirez and Rogers dealt with Leo, she slipped past them into the shed. "Jace?" she called.

"I'm over here."

She turned toward the sound of his voice as he emerged from beneath a brown tarp. Something loosened in her chest as he moved toward her, no sign of blood or injury, only a smear of dirt across one cheek. "Where's Leo?" he asked, looking toward the open shed door.

"Rogers and Ramirez have him. What's going on?"

He switched on a penlight and shone the beam on an opening in the far wall. "There's a workshop in there full of bomb-making materials," he said. "Or there was, until Leo started moving them out."

"Leo is the bomber?" The knowledge didn't surprise her, but it did disappoint her. Leo had seemed more pathetic than evil to her. Yet he had murdered two people.

Ramirez joined them in the shed. "Rogers has Leo cuffed in our vehicle and the local police are on their way," she said.

"What was in those boxes?" Laura asked.

"Electronics, wiring, fuses and explosives,"

Jace said. "Everything you'd need to make a bomb. Lots of bombs, I'd guess."

"Has Leo said anything?" Jace asked.

"Only that he didn't kill anyone. Then he asked for his lawyer and shut up." Ramirez shrugged. "We'll get the whole story, eventually." She looked Jace up and down. "You okay?"

"Yeah." He gestured toward the shed. "I saw Leo in here moving around and got curious. I came to get a closer look, then got trapped when he started moving in and out. I texted Laura for help."

"He didn't resist," Ramirez said. "I don't even think he was armed. We'll wrap things up here. You two should go before your cover is blown."

They headed back toward the truck and the van. "You could have arrested him yourself," Laura said. "Why did you call me? To preserve your cover?"

"That, and to make sure there were plenty of witnesses to catch him red-handed with those bomb-making supplies." He grinned. "I wouldn't want anyone to accuse me of taking short cuts and jeopardizing the case."

She wanted to give him a good shove. She also wanted to throw her arms around him and tell him how glad she was that he was safe. Instead, she moved away from him, toward her truck, before she let emotion get the better of her.

"I DIDN'T KILL anyone." Leo Elgin, in an orange jumpsuit with PRISONER in large white letters stenciled across the front and back, sat across the table from Ana and Rogers at the Mayville Police Department, his wrists and ankles shackled, his court-appointed attorney on one side of him, a police officer on the other.

"Leo, we can match materials we found in your workshop to both the bombs that exploded at Stroud Pharmaceuticals," Ana said. "The bombs that killed Lydia Green and Angela Dupree."

"Did Angela or Lydia put that poison in the Stomach Soothers?" Leo asked, more desperate than defiant. "The poison that killed my mother?"

"Is that what you think?" Ana leaned across the table toward him. "That Lydia and Angela killed your mother, so you planted the bombs to kill them?"

"Did they?"

"We haven't found anything to link either of them to the poisoned medication," Rogers said.

Leo buried his face in his hands and began to sob.

"My client is clearly distraught," said the attorney, a motherly woman in her midfifties, with silver curls and tortoise-shell bifocals. "He has nothing else to say to you at this time."

Ana and Rogers rose. "We have more questions for you, Leo," Ana said. "We know you made those bombs. That makes you guilty of murder, whether you put them at the plant or not. If you didn't, as you say, kill Lydia and Angela, then who did?"

She followed Rogers from the room. The chief of police, Gary Simonson, met them at the end of the hall. "Did you get anything out of him?" he asked.

Rogers shook his head. "But Leo made those bombs. I don't have any doubt about that."

"But did he plant them at the factory?" Ana asked.

"Maybe." Rogers rubbed his jaw, stubble rasping against his palm. Like Ana, he had had only a couple of hours of sleep in the past two days, and his eyes looked sunken in his handsome face. "Probably. He had his mother's key and pass to get in. She had worked there for years, so he probably knew his way around."

"But who poisoned the medication?" Ana asked. "Was it really Lydia and Angela?"

"Is that what he's saying?" Simonson asked. "That he killed those women because they poisoned his mother?"

"We'll take a closer look at them, but nothing in the backgrounds of any of the Stroud employees points to a motive for the poisonings," Rogers said. "Both Angela and Lydia had worked for Stroud for years, with good reports. They didn't have so much as a traffic ticket on their records."

"He asked us if they put the poison in the Stomach Soothers," Ana said. "As if he wanted us to confirm what he thought." She frowned. "Though really, he sounded unsure. And he kept insisting he didn't kill anyone."

"The bombs he made killed them," Rogers said. "That makes him a murderer."

"You and I know that, but maybe Leo wasn't clear on that," she said. "Maybe he made the bombs for someone else to use. Or he thought they would be used for some other purpose." The more she considered Leo's words and reactions, the more this idea fit.

Her phone rang. She checked the display. "It's Maynard," she said. "I'd better take it."

She moved down the hall, leaving Rogers with the police chief. "Hey Hendrick," she answered the call from the team's technology expert. "What have you got for me?"

"I've been through all the video you sent from Stroud Pharmaceuticals' security cameras. All of it," he emphasized. "Three weeks' worth of footage, inside and out."

"And?" She pressed the phone more tightly to her ear.

"There were hundreds of people going in and out of that place, but all of them were either employees, vendors, or family members of employees. My team was able to identify every single person on those feeds."

"Great job." She tried to put more enthusiasm into her voice than she felt. "Anything significant?"

"The only thing significant is who *isn't* there," Hendrick said.

Her stomach churned. "Who isn't there?"

"Leo Elgin isn't there. Not inside the buildings. Not outside the buildings. We've got good footage of the areas around both bombing sites and Leo was never there."

Rogers joined her. She met his questioning gaze and shook her head. "Thanks, Hendrick," she said, and ended the call.

"Leo Elgin isn't in any of the security footage from Stroud," she said. "He may have made those two bombs, but he didn't plant them."

"So he has an accomplice who works for Stroud?" Rogers asked.

"He must have. But who?"

"There's only a couple of people we know he's met with since he got back in town," Rogers said. "Let's get Parker Stroud in here and talk to him."

Chapter Eleven

At work Wednesday, Parker, still sporting a few bruises but otherwise seemingly unhurt, asked Laura for more reports. "Why are you looking at everything from the first quarter?" she asked when she delivered the first batch to his desk.

"Not that it's any of your business, but I'm working on a new design that will make us even more efficient and productive."

"I heard there might be another bomb," she said. "Do you think that's true?"

His eyes narrowed. "Who told you that?"

She shrugged. "I just heard some people talk."

"Haven't you heard talk is cheap?"

"But do you think there could be another bomb?"

"I don't know. Maybe."

"But why?"

"Because someone is out to destroy this business and my family." She heard no anger behind his words, only bleak resignation. "Now get out of here and leave me to work in peace."

She left and remained at her desk the rest of the morning, having finally hacked into Stroud Pharmaceuticals' financial records for the past two quarters. On the surface the reports were competent, but the deeper she dug, the messier things got. Was Virginia Elgin that incompetent, or had someone conveniently deleted chunks of data from the files?

Parker wasn't at his desk when Ramirez and Rogers arrived after lunch and asked to speak to him. "He stepped away half an hour ago," Laura said. "He didn't tell me where he was going."

"Any idea where we should look?" Rogers asked.

"Let me see if I can find him," she said, and hurried away. Better she should go roaming through the plant than two known federal agents, who would raise alarms and have everyone competing to come up with ever-wilder explanations for their presence.

When the coffee room and his mother's office showed no signs of Parker, she headed for the factory floor and found him with Jace, of all people, discussing a malfunction with the fill machine. Jace gave her a warm smile. "Hey, sweetheart," he said.

She ignored him and focused on Parker. "There are two FBI agents here who want to talk to you," she said.

He masked his alarm so quickly she might not

have noticed if she hadn't been watching for it. "Tell them I'm unavailable," he said.

"I can't do that," she protested. "They're the FBI."

"And I don't have time to talk to them. Tell them you couldn't find me. You don't know where I am." He turned to Jace. "That goes for you, too," he said.

"Yes, sir." Jace met Laura's gaze, one eyebrow raised in question.

"Yes, sir," she said, and turned away.

Back at the office, she found Ramirez and Rogers still standing. "He's on the factory floor," she said. "Packaging. But my guess is he'll be headed for the parking lot soon. If you hurry, you can catch him."

Ten minutes later, Ramirez and Rogers followed Parker back into the office. He headed for his private sanctum without a glance in Laura's direction. Ramirez nodded at her and followed Parker and Rogers, but she left the door open a scant half inch.

Laura moved to the door. "Why were you running away from us?" Rogers asked.

"I wasn't running," Parker said. "I had an appointment to meet our regional sales manager. If you want to speak with me, you can schedule a meeting with my secretary."

"This can't wait," Rogers said. "We want to

talk to you about your relationship with Leo Elgin."

"I don't know what you're talking about." Parker's voice was forceful and sure. He was a good bluffer. But not good enough.

"You know Leo Elgin," Ramirez said.

"Yes." Parker's chair creaked. "His mother worked for us before her tragic death. And Leo and I went to the same high school."

"The two of you are friends," Ramirez said.

"We're acquaintances. And what difference does that make, anyway? I know a lot of people."

"Leo Elgin was arrested early this morning, and charged with manufacturing the explosive devices that killed Lydia Green and Angela Dupree," Rogers said.

Silence, then Ramirez's voice. "Mr. Stroud? Are you all right?"

When Parker finally spoke, his voice had lost all its energy and defiance. "Leo planted those bombs here? But why?"

"Why don't you take a moment to pull yourself together," Ramirez said. She moved to the doorway. "Mr. Stroud needs some water," she said.

Laura filled a paper cup from a dispenser across the room and brought it to her. "What happened?" she asked, her voice low.

"The news of Leo's arrest clearly shocked him," Ramirez said. "I thought he was going to pass out."

She moved into Parker's office once more, still leaving the door ajar. "Mr. Stroud, how well did you know Ms. Green and Ms. Dupree?" Rogers asked.

"They were family friends as well as employees, but my mother knows—knew—both of them better than I did." Parker paused, perhaps to sip water, then added, "I'm still upset about their deaths. Such a waste."

"Do you know of any reason either woman might have wanted to sabotage the Stomach Soothers?" Rogers asked. "Could they have put the poison in the tablets?"

"Angela and Lydia?"

"One or both of them," Ramirez said.

"No! Why would they? They were good women. Lydia taught Sunday school. Angela and my mother were best friends. Besides all that, neither of them came near the factory operations. I don't see when or how they could have introduced the poison into the tablets." Another pause. "Are you suggesting Leo planted the bombs to kill those women because he believed they were responsible for Gini's death?"

"We're exploring a number of possible motives," Rogers said. "Right now, we want to know more about your dealings with Leo Elgin."

"I didn't have any dealings with Leo."

"We have witnesses who have seen you together on at least two occasions recently," Rogers said.

Parker's voice remained calm. Reasonable. "We've run into each other a couple of times since he returned to town and I've offered my condolences, that's all."

"What about the money you gave him?" Rogers asked.

"What money?" Parker's voice was sharp, with a hint of outrage.

"The money you had your girlfriend, Merry Winger, deliver to Leo last Saturday," Rogers said. "The day of Gini Elgin's memorial service. Ms. Winger says you asked her to leave the service, drive to the Elgin home, and give an envelope of money to Leo Elgin."

"My family wanted to contribute to the funeral costs. Leo was too proud to take the money when I originally offered it, but I thought if Merry delivered it he would accept it, and I was right."

"You were already paying for the catering for the reception after the service," Ramirez said.

"Yes, but we wanted to do more," Parker said. "Gini was a beloved, long-time employee of Stroud Pharmaceuticals and while we didn't cause her death, we feel terrible that one of our products was the instrument of her demise."

The instrument of her demise? Really? Laura wondered if he had practiced delivering that line.

"What do you think you're doing?"

She turned to find Merry in the doorway. "Two FBI agents are in there questioning Parker," Laura said, keeping her voice low.

Merry's eyes widened and she hurried to join Laura by Parker's door. "What does the FBI want with Parker?" she whispered.

Laura led her back to the desk. "They asked about the money you delivered to Leo Elgin the day of the funeral," she said.

Merry scowled. "What does that have to do with anything?"

"Why did you leave Gini's funeral to deliver that money to Leo?" Laura asked.

"Parker asked me to do it." She dropped into the chair in front of the desk. "He begged me to do it, really. Finally, he agreed to buy me a pair of diamond earrings if I would do it for him." She fingered the glittering earrings at her lobes.

Laura leaned back against the front of the desk. "But why did he want you to go to Leo's during the funeral?" she asked.

"He said he didn't want to embarrass Leo." She looked toward the office door. "What did Parker say when the feds asked him about the envelope?"

"He said the money was to help pay for Gini's funeral."

Merry raised her hands, clearly exasperated. "Why couldn't Parker tell me that? He just said to give the envelope to Leo and not to ask more questions. He didn't even tell me it was full of money—to find that out, I had to peek."

"What did you think when you saw the money?" Laura asked.

"I was worried Parker was buying drugs off Leo or something."

"How much money was it?"

"A lot. There was a thick stack of hundred-dollar bills."

Laura crossed her arms over her chest. "Would a funeral cost that much?"

"I don't know. I never had to pay for one. But I've always heard how expensive they are."

"Do you think Parker is doing drugs?" Laura asked.

"Well, no," Merry said. "I mean, when we go out he hardly ever has more than one beer. He doesn't smoke, either." She smiled. "It's one of the things I like about him. He doesn't really have any bad habits. If you ask him, he'll say his only vice is that he works too hard."

Laura hadn't seen much evidence of that, considering how often her boss came in late or left early. "Why would Parker give Leo money for his mother's funeral?" she asked.

"Because he felt terrible about Gini's death. He really did. I was with him when he got the news that she died. He went paper white and I thought he might pass out. He kept saying 'no, no, no.' I didn't know he was that close to Gini, but she had worked here a long time, so I guess he thought of her like an aunt."

Or maybe Parker had paid Leo to keep quiet about something. Or to stop publicly blaming Stroud Pharmaceuticals for his mother's death. The bad publicity surrounding the poisonings had hurt the business and though there were signs of things improving, it would take a long time to fully recover from this. Paying for the funeral might be an acceptable way to buy Leo's silence and cooperation.

The door to Parker's office opened and Parker, Ramirez and Rogers emerged. "If you think of anything else that might help us in our investigation, please call," Ramirez said.

Parker said nothing, and when Rogers and Ramirez were gone, Merry rushed to his side. "What did they want?" she asked.

"They've arrested Leo in connection with the two bombings here at the plant," Parker said. He looked older, the lines around his eyes and mouth deeper, his skin tinged with an unhealthy pallor.

"Leo planted those bombs!" Merry's voice rose. "Leo, who wouldn't say boo to a fly?"

"They think he was working with someone here at the plant," Parker said. "Someone who helped him gain access."

"But why?" Merry asked. "I mean, his mother dies, so he's going to take out two more random people? That doesn't even make sense."

"Grief can do strange things to people." Parker fixed Merry with a chilly gaze. "Can you think of anyone here who might be helping Leo?"

"No! Why are you looking at me that way?" She put a hand to her chest. "I certainly didn't help him. I think he's creepy."

"You just said he was harmless," Laura said.

"Well, yeah. Harmless, but creepy. As far as I know, he doesn't even have friends. At least, not here."

"They asked a lot of questions about the money I gave Leo." Parker's expression grew more frigid. "What were you doing, talking to the FBI about me?"

Merry took a step back. "They questioned me. I couldn't not answer their questions, could I? I mean, they're the FBI!"

"You should have kept your mouth shut."

"Parker, I —"

He put a hand on her shoulder and steered her to the door. "You need to go now." He opened the door, pushed her into the hallway, then shut the door in her face.

She left and Laura moved back to her desk. "I know you were listening at the door," Parker said.

"I was curious what they wanted with you."

"Are those the two who interviewed you and your husband?"

"Yes."

"Did they ask you if you knew Leo?"

"No."

"Don't worry, they probably will. They're not making any progress in the case, so they're grasping at straws." He started out of the office.

"Where are you going?" she asked. When he glared at her, she added, "In case anyone is looking for you."

"I'm going back to work. You should do the same."

He had been gone less than a minute when the phone on Laura's desk rang. "Hello?" she answered.

"I just saw Ramirez and Rogers leave," Jace said. "What happened up there?"

"They questioned Parker."

"And?"

She glanced toward the open door and lowered her voice. "Apparently, the envelope Merry delivered to Leo the day of his mother's funeral was full of hundred-dollar bills, from Parker."

Jace whistled. "What was the money for?"

"Parker says it was to pay for Gini's funeral. He had Merry deliver it during the service to avoid embarrassing Leo."

"Do you believe him?"

"I don't know. What does Leo say about what happened?"

"Leo isn't talking."

"Maybe we should make a deal with him—the

name of his partner for a lighter sentence or reduction of charges."

"He's responsible for the deaths of two people." Jace sounded outraged. "And we caught him red-handed with the bomb-making materials. We're not going to make any deals with him."

"Maybe we should. In case there's another bomb."

"He's not going to be making any more bombs in prison," Jace said.

"There was a lot of material in that root cellar," Laura said. "Enough for a dozen more bombs. What if he made more than two to begin with? What if there's another one out there, ready to go off any minute now?"

Chapter Twelve

"We're not getting anywhere with Elgin." Rogers's frustration threaded his voice. "He's scared, and we're trying to use that to get him to cooperate, but so far he hasn't given us anything."

Jace tucked the phone under his chin and began turning the burgers that sizzled on the grill in the shade of the catalpa tree behind the trailer. "Did you get anything out of Parker Stroud this morning?"

"He's hiding something, but a lot of people are," Rogers said. "Maybe the money he gave Elgin really was for Gini's funeral. Right now we can't prove it wasn't."

"Laura thinks Elgin might have built more than the two bombs. There was enough material in that root cellar for that."

"Maybe. We're working on tracking all his movements for the last month. You know this isn't a fast process."

Right. But sometimes the Bureau was too methodical for Jace's taste. While they dotted all the *i*'s and crossed all the *t*'s, someone else could get hurt—or killed.

He ended the call and thought about going into the house to find Laura. But that would mean leaving the burgers to possibly burn. Instead, he took his phone out again and texted her. Heard from D. Come out here for update and dinner.

Five long minutes passed before the back door opened and Laura stepped out, balancing a stack of plates and silverware and a tray of condiments. She wore shorts that showed off smooth, toned legs and he had to force himself not to stare. Fortunately, she was too focused on her task to notice his reaction. "What did Rogers say?" she asked and set her burden on the picnic table near the grill.

"They're not getting anything out of Elgin."

She settled at the picnic table. "If a suspect won't talk to us, it's usually because they're more afraid of someone else than they are of us," she said.

They had changed out of their work clothes into shorts and T-shirts, and it was surprisingly pleasant in the shaded backyard, almost relaxing, except for the case that nagged at them. Jace topped the burgers with cheese and waited for it to melt. "Who's he afraid of? His partner?"

"That would be my guess," she said.

He slid the burgers onto a plate and joined her at the table. Guesses were fine for steering the investigation in a likely direction, but what they needed now was proof. He didn't have to point that out to Laura. She had been with the Bureau longer than he had, and she seemed much more comfortable with the way they worked. He admired her smarts and dedication, if not her play-by-the-rules attitude.

"I've found something worth looking into," she said.

The way she delivered this news—oh so casual—had him on high alert. "What did you find?"

"I've been digging through Parker Stroud's financial records." She spread mustard on her burger and arranged lettuce and tomato.

Jace sat across from her and focused on his own burger. "What did you find?"

"I found a secret bank account, under the name Steven Parker. With a balance of $10 million."

Jace whistled. "Where did Parker get $10 million to stash away?"

"I wondered that, too," she said. "The money began showing up about two years ago—a few thousand here, ten thousand there. But the pace of deposits has really accelerated in the past six months."

"That doesn't sound like an inheritance or a lucky investment," Jace said.

"No. And here's something else even more interesting." She picked up her burger. "The money isn't just going in. It's going out, to the tune of two payments of $50,000 each over the past two weeks."

"Is he buying up property or other investments?" Jace asked.

"Let me give you another clue. The first payment was made three days after the first victim was poisoned by Stomach Soothers. Two days after Gini Elgin died."

Their eyes met, a look of triumph lighting hers. "You think someone is blackmailing Parker because he poisoned the Stomach Soothers," Jace said.

"I think it would be a good idea to ask him, don't you?"

Jace glanced at his plate. "Can I finish my burger first? I mean, he's not likely to run, is he?"

"He's at a Rotary Club meeting, of all things, tonight. And he's supposed to be at work in the morning. I haven't seen any sign of him wanting to run. So I think we're good. I'll pass this info on to Ramirez and Rogers and let them handle it."

"That's great work," Jace said.

Her cheeks went a shade pinker, until she took a big bite and chewed, looking thoughtful. With her hair down around her shoulders and no makeup, she looked young and soft. Not weak, but…touchable.

She took a long sip from a bottle of a local microbrew and sighed. "It would fit so neatly if we found out Parker had planted the poison in those tablets and was setting off these bombs," she said. "But he's given every indication that he's desperate to keep the business going—so why do something like planting poison in the company's top product? It's going to take years to recover from the bad press. And from what I can tell from looking at the company financials, there's a very real risk they won't pull out."

"See anything alarming in the company books?" Jace asked.

"Only that they're a mess. Gini Elgin may have been a wonderful person, but she kept terrible records. It would require months of close work to straighten out completely. I've only been able to look at them in my spare time."

"I agree that Parker doesn't have a good motive for the poisoning," Jace said. "So where does that leave us?"

"I don't think Angela or Lydia did it," she said. "There's no motive and even less opportunity. They both worked in the offices, not on the factory floor. And I don't think Leo did it."

"Maybe he didn't do it intending to kill his mother," Jace said. "Her death was an accident."

Laura shook her head. "Leo was in Nashville when the poisonings began. He hadn't been back to Mayville in four months."

"That we know of. It's only a six-hour drive

and only a couple hours on a plane. He could be here and back in well under a day."

"I still don't think he did it."

"Then who did?"

She set aside her partially eaten burger. "Maybe we've been looking at this all wrong," she said. "Maybe the poisoning didn't have anything to do with Stroud. Maybe some nutso contaminated the pills after they were placed on store shelves—like the Tylenol case."

In Chicago in 1982, someone had removed bottles of Tylenol from store shelves and contaminated the pills with potassium cyanide. Seven people had died, and requirements for tamper-resistant packaging had been instituted as a result.

"We haven't found any evidence of tampering with the safety seals on the bottles of Stomach Soothers or the boxes containing the bottles," Jace said. "The forensic people examined every container they could get their hands on with X-rays. And how do we account for the missing bottles? They never made it from the factory to a store."

"Which brings us back to the idea that someone working in the factory slipped the ricin into the bottles during the packaging process?" She picked up her burger and took another bite.

"That person might be Elgin's partner," Jace said. "The one who planted the bomb. But what's the motive?"

"To destroy the company? Or maybe the Stroud family?"

"It seems like if you had an enemy who hated you that much, you'd know about it," Jace said. "And the Strouds insist they have no idea who is doing this."

"People lie," Laura said.

"They do, but we ought to be able to spot the lies."

They fell into silence, finishing their burgers and beer, letting the late afternoon stillness wash over them, a hot breeze fluttering their paper napkins and stirring the ends of Laura's hair. They were seated across from each other, not touching, yet the moment felt intimate. She pushed her empty plate away and sat back. "I like it here a lot more than I thought I would," she said, glancing around the weedy backyard, with its scraggly line of bright yellow daylilies along the fence and the arching branches of oak and catalpa providing shade.

"It has a way of getting to you," he said. "Life here moves at a slower pace, the people are a little less guarded, the landscape is so lush." He felt the pull of settling into old routines, and he couldn't say he liked it.

"How is your family?"

The question caught him off guard. He shrugged. "They're my family." He kept in touch by phone, but he hadn't let anyone know he was working so nearby. "Like all families, they do things that I love and things that drive me crazy."

She leaned toward him, elbows on the picnic table. "Like what?"

He shook his head. "They don't understand why I ever left home. Ambition isn't something they admire. It's just another word for 'getting above yourself.' They judge me for my choices, but if I do the same to them I must think I'm better than them." He shrugged. "I can't change them. I don't try anymore, and maybe that's a good thing. What about your family?"

"There's just my dad. My mom died when I was ten."

"That's rough. Do you have any brothers and sisters?"

She shook her head. "And no close family. We moved a lot, so my dad and I relied on each other."

"Still, it must have been hard, always being the new kid."

She sat up straighter. "It taught me to adapt, to learn how to fit in."

He studied her a moment. Maybe it was that second beer loosening his tongue—or maybe he just wanted to risk being honest with her. "I think it taught you to keep your distance, to not get too involved."

She frowned. He held up a hand and said, "Don't look at me that way. I didn't say there was necessarily anything wrong with that."

"You think I'm cold." Pain clouded her blue eyes. "It's all right. You wouldn't be the first to say so."

"Oh, you ought to know by now that I don't think you're cold." He moved around the table and slid onto the bench beside her. She watched him, wary, but didn't resist when he pulled her into his arms and kissed her.

You shouldn't be *kissing him. It isn't professional. It isn't part of your mission.*

Shut up. I'm not a robot. I have a life outside the mission. Laura shut her eyes, shutting out the nagging voice inside of herself—a voice that too often sounded like her father—and surrendered to the pure pleasure of kissing Jace. The pressure of his lips on hers sent sparks of awareness dancing along her nerves, awakening desires that had lain dormant too long. She leaned into his embrace, done with fighting her attraction to him.

When she finally pulled away, the heated longing in his eyes made her toes curl. "What are you thinking?" he asked.

"That we should take this inside." She stood and tugged him to his feet. Grinning now, he let her lead him into the house. When the door was closed behind them, she kissed him again, his back against the wall, his hunger matching her own.

His skin smelled of pine and soap, and the faint whiff of the barbecue smoke. He tasted of salt and cinnamon as she traced her tongue along his jaw. He groaned when she nipped at his throat, and slid his hands around to cup her bottom and snug her more firmly against him. Oh, yes—those shorts of his didn't leave any doubt how he felt about her. She smiled up at him. "Want to try out my new bed?"

"I thought you'd never ask."

She hurried through the awkwardness of shedding her clothes, sneaking looks as he took off his shorts, shirt and underwear, her heart speeding up in appreciation for his naked body. She had seen him a few times in the gym at headquarters, but she'd never admired him with the same interest before. He had plenty of sexy muscles to go with the brains and bravery that had attracted her in the first place.

They crawled into bed and moved into each other's arms, a sigh escaping her as she pressed her body to his. His hands slid up her thighs, calluses dragging on her smooth skin. The heat of his fingers pressed into her soft flesh and delved into the wetness between her legs.

She moaned, the sound muffled by the liquid heat of his tongue tangling with her own. He dipped his head to kiss her naked breasts—butterfly touches of his lips over and around the swelling flesh, then latching on to her sensitive, distended nipple, sucking hard, the pulling sensation reaching all the way to her groin, where she tightened around his plunging finger.

He stretched out beside her, kissing her deeply while his hands caressed, stroking her breasts and tracing the curve of her hips and stomach, never lingering too long at any one place. She arched toward him, anxious with need. "Shh," he soothed. "We don't have to hurry." He patted her stomach. "I'll be right back," he said, then rose and padded out of the room.

Curious, she propped herself on her elbow and enjoyed the view of him leaving the room. When he returned holding a condom packet aloft, she laughed and opened her arms to welcome him back.

The sight of him sheathing himself left her breathless. He levered himself over her, and she raised her knees and spread her legs to allow him access, but he only smiled and slid down her body, his tongue tracing the curve of her breasts, the ridges of her ribs and the hollow of her navel. By the time he plunged his tongue into her wet channel, she was quivering with need, half-mad with lust. She buried her fingers in his hair as he stroked her clit with his tongue.

"What do you want?" he whispered, his voice rough, as if he was fighting for control.

"I want you." Her voice rose at the last word, as he levered himself over her and entered her, his fingers digging into her bottom. The sensation of him filling her, stretching her, moving inside her, made her dizzy. "Don't stop," she gasped. "Please don't stop."

"I won't stop. I promise I won't stop."

He drove hard, but held her so gently, his fingers stroking, caressing, even as his hips pumped. She slid her hands around to cup his ass, marveling at the feel of his muscles contracting and relaxing with each powerful thrust.

He slipped his hand between them and began to fondle her clit, each deft move sending the tension within her coiling tighter. He kissed the soft flesh at the base of her throat. "I want to make it good for you," he murmured. "So good."

She sensed him holding back, waiting for her. When her climax overtook her, he swallowed her cries, then mingled them with his own as his release shuddered through them both.

MUCH LATER, THE dull buzz of Jace's phone vibrating across the bedside table pulled him from sleep. Eyes half-open, he groped for the device and swiped to answer it. "Hello?"

"Jace, it's Ramirez." The tension in Ramirez's voice snapped him awake. He swung his legs up to sit on the side of the bed as Laura propped herself up beside him.

"What's happened?" he asked.

"There's been another explosion at Stroud Pharmaceuticals," she said. "It's bad. That's all I know. Just...bad."

Chapter Thirteen

The chaos at Stroud Pharmaceuticals overflowed into the streets, so that blocks away, Jace maneuvered the truck through crowds of people, some openly weeping, others agitated or merely excited to know what was happening. The strobe of the light bars atop police cruisers looked garish against the soft pink and orange of sunrise.

He parked three blocks from the Stroud compound, unable to go farther, and he and Laura walked the rest of the way, joining a parade of Stroud employees headed in that direction. "I swear I heard the bomb go off," said a woman named Janice, who worked in packaging. "I had just let the dog out and I heard it. I thought it was someone hunting."

Police and county sheriff's vehicles formed a barricade at the entrance to the factory and offices. Media trucks ringed the area, satellite dishes pointed to the sky. Jace thought he spotted Rogers talking to one of the cops, and then he was swallowed up in the confusion. "I heard Mr. Stroud—Mr. Steve—is dead," Barb Falk said.

"Mr. Parker is in the hospital," Phyllis Neighbors added, blotting tears from her eyes with her index fingers.

"This is so awful," a woman Jace didn't know said. "It just keeps happening. I'm too afraid to go back in there again. Not with some nut job trying to blow up everybody."

"There's Donna." Laura tugged at Jace's sleeve and he followed her gaze to where Donna Stroud, dressed in a navy pantsuit, stood surrounded by reporters, microphones and recorders all but obscuring her face.

Jace and Laura shoved forward, ignoring the grumbling of those they displaced, until they reached the ring of reporters.

Donna Stroud's face looked drained of blood, and her voice was strained. "We will stop production for the next few days out of respect for my husband, and to protect the safety of our employees," she said.

"Do you have any idea who did this?"

"What about the suspect the police have in custody? Do they have the wrong man?"

"Why hasn't the FBI stopped this?" The reporters fired questions at the dazed woman.

"Why haven't we stopped this?" Laura muttered. Anguish haunted her gaze and anger weighted her words. "I knew there were more bombs out there. We should have insisted they close the factory."

She kept her voice low, barely audible even to Jace, but still he put his arm around her and turned her away from the reporters. "We could have insisted the Strouds close the plant, but everyone from the state legislator to local officials to the Strouds themselves would have refused," he said.

"They don't have any choice now," she said. She scanned the crowd. "Most of the employees are probably too frightened to return to work."

"Let me through. I have to talk to Donna. I have to find out about Parker."

The crowd parted and Merry, wet hair straggling around her shoulders, eyes swollen from crying, staggered forward. She clutched at Laura's shoulder. "I was in the shower when a friend called to tell me what had happened," she half sobbed. "Parker's in the hospital, but when I went down there, they wouldn't let me see him!" Her voice rose in a wail that attracted the attention of the reporters and Donna.

Laura took the distraught young woman's arm and led her away. Jace followed, shielding them from the curious stares of those around them. "When was the last time you saw Parker?" Laura asked.

Merry sniffed. "He spent the night at my place," she said. "But he left really early this morning.

His mom called about some problem with Parker's dad. He had to leave to deal with that."

"What was the problem?" Jace asked.

"I don't know. He just said he had to go deal with his dad."

"What time was this?" Laura asked.

"Early. About five o'clock." She yawned. "I went back to bed. That was the last I heard until my friend Margo called me about seven." Her face crumpled again. "She said Parker was hurt in the explosion, but no one at the hospital will tell me anything."

"Merry, pull yourself together. Parker is going to be all right." Donna Stroud moved in and put her arm around the weeping woman. "He had surgery to remove some shrapnel from his legs, but he's going to be okay."

"What happened?" Laura asked. "Merry said Parker left early this morning to help his dad?"

The lines around Donna's eyes deepened. "I woke up early this morning and Steve wasn't in bed. I realized what had woken me was the garage door opening and closing. He does that sometimes, gets restless and goes for a drive. No matter how well I think I hide the car keys, he always seems to find them."

"Where does he go?" Jace asked.

Guilt pinched her features. "Often, he comes here, to his office. That's why I called Parker. He's better at reasoning with his dad, persuading him to return home. But apparently when they got here…" She covered her mouth with one hand, choking back a sob.

"Is there anything I can do to help?" Laura asked. Something in her voice made Jace think she wasn't asking merely as a way of finding out more information, but out of genuine concern for Mrs. Stroud.

"I may need you to retrieve some reports and things from Parker's office later," Donna said. "Though I know that isn't really your job."

"For now, it is my job," Laura said, with a warning glance at Merry.

Merry seemed not to have even heard. She clutched Donna's arm. "Mrs. Stroud, was there a note?" she asked.

"I don't think now is the time to talk about that," Donna said.

Merry frowned at Jace and Laura. "Don't tell me you haven't heard about the notes from the bomber. I thought everyone knew about them by now."

"We have heard some rumors," Laura said.

Donna sighed, then reached into her pocket and took out a crumpled envelope. "This was on my desk when I got in this morning."

Jace took the envelope, handling it carefully. It was different from the others in that this one had no stamp or postmark. "What does the note inside say?" Jace asked.

"It says 'three down, three more soon.'" Donna took the note from him and returned it to her pocket. "I'll give this to Agent Ramirez or Agent Rogers when I see them," she said. "But for now, I need to focus on handling the plant closure and taking care of my family. And I need to deal with these reporters." She turned away, head up, shoulders back, a woman prepared to do battle.

"How long is the plant going to be closed?" Merry asked.

Jace had almost forgotten Merry. Now she inserted herself between him and Laura, tears and hair both drying in the early morning heat. The crowd around them had thinned somewhat, many employees drifting back to their homes or vehicles, or gathering at the far end of the parking lot to watch from a distance.

"I guess they'll keep the plant closed until they figure out who's responsible for the bombs," he said.

"They arrested Leo," Merry said. "I thought he's the one who did this. It's no secret he blames the Strouds for killing his mother."

"Leo was in jail when this bomb exploded," Jace said.

"Maybe he planted it before he was arrested."

"Maybe." None of the other explosives had been equipped with a timing mechanism, but maybe this one was different.

"I'm going to tell Donna she needs to call the

hospital and let me in to see Parker," Merry said, and started after the older woman.

Laura moved in close to Jace once more. "We need to get to the hospital and talk to Parker," she said.

"How are we going to do that without blowing our cover?" he asked.

"I'm his admin. I'll say how concerned I am for him and is there anything I can do to help his mother at this difficult time."

He put his arm around her. "Has anyone ever told you you'd make a good secret agent?"

She made a face, but didn't move away. The public display of affection fit with their cover, but Jace hoped there was more than that to her desire to be close to him.

THEY HEARD PARKER long before they reached his room, his voice reverberating down the hospital corridor. "I told you I need something stronger for this pain. You need to get hold of that doctor now. I don't want to hear any more of your lame excuses."

"I see the explosion didn't do anything to dampen his charm," Jace said.

"At least he's awake and lucid enough," Laura said. They halted outside Parker's door as a young black man in blue scrubs hurried into the hallway. He scarcely glanced at them as he headed toward the nurse's station. Laura tapped on the door.

"Come in!" Parker barked.

Laura pushed open the door. "Mr. Stroud, it's me, Laura. My husband is with me."

Parker, his hair uncombed and day-old stubble softening the line of his jaw, looked younger and slightly vulnerable. Or maybe it was the faded hospital gown and network of tubes and monitors that added to his air of helplessness. "How did you get in here?" he asked. "I told them no visitors."

"No one said anything to us," Laura said. Security clearly wasn't a priority at this small hospital. Jace had popped the lock on the outside door leading to the stairway at the end of this hall and they had been able to stroll in, bypassing the nurse's station and any other authority figures. "Is there anything I can do for you?" Laura asked, approaching the bed.

"You can find my doctor and tell him I need something stronger for pain than aspirin."

"What happened?" Laura asked. "Your mother said she sent you to look for your father."

"So you've been talking to her." His expression softened. "How is she?"

"She's staying tough," Jace said. "In shock, I think, but handling the press."

"She announced she's shutting down the factory until the police catch who did this," Laura said. "I was sorry to hear about your father."

"The stupid old fool." There was no heat behind the words. Parker slumped against the pillows. "He likes to sneak away and come to the office. It doesn't hurt anything. He types up memos or prints out reports. He doesn't even know what day it is much of the time, but he's harmless. But Mom worries, so I agreed to go get him and bring him home."

He fell silent and they waited, the silence punctuated by the beep of monitors and the whirring of the automatic blood pressure cuff.

"What happened?" Laura prompted.

"I saw his car in the parking lot, and then I spotted him going into the building," Parker said. "I followed him and he was just unlocking the door to his office when I reached him. I called out his name and he turned to me. Then everything just disintegrated." His face crumpled. "He was smiling, like he was so happy to see me."

Laura plucked a tissue from the box by the bed and passed it to him. They waited while he wept. When he had pulled himself together, Jace asked, "Did you see anything else when you got to the plant this morning? Any other cars in the lot, or anyone hanging around?"

Parker grimaced. "You sound like a cop."

"I'm curious. Who wouldn't be?"

"I didn't see anyone," Parker said. "It was early and most people were still in bed. I only passed one car on the way to the plant, and that was Phil Dorsey, on his way to open the café for breakfast."

"Merry said you were with her last night," Laura said.

"So you talked to her already," Parker said.

"She was at the plant," Laura said. "She was upset that hospital personnel wouldn't let her see you."

"I couldn't deal with her distress right now."

"But you were with her last night?" Jace asked.

"I was." He laughed, a bitter sound. "Don't ever play poker, Laura dear. Your opinion of me shows all too clearly."

Only because I wasn't trying to hide it, she thought.

"You think I'm taking advantage of the poor girl, stringing her along and taking what I want. Believe me, she's getting what she wants, too."

"What does she want?" Laura asked.

"Money. The status of being associated with my name. It may not mean much to you, but in this town, the Strouds are about as big as they get."

"Merry believes you're going to marry her," Laura said.

"I've never proposed. She doesn't have a ring."

But you haven't told her it will never happen.

"Were you with Merry all night?" Jace asked.

"Yes. Though that's none of your business."

The door opened and an older woman in a skirt and blouse, a stethoscope around her neck, entered. "Mr. Stroud, I understand you're experiencing some pain."

"It's about time you got here. And yes, I'm experiencing pain. A lot of it."

Laura and Jace took that as their cue to leave. She waited until they were in the truck before she spoke. "He's terrified," she said. "That's what's behind his bluster."

"He was lucky he wasn't killed," Jace said. "His father was. That's enough to terrify anyone."

"I was almost sure he was Leo's partner," she said. The two of them had been seen together several times, and Parker was so circumspect about their relationship."

"But now you're not so sure?" Jace prompted.

"No. Why would he kill his father and risk his own life?"

"If he killed his father, he'd be more likely to inherit the business sooner," Jace said. "He hasn't made a secret of wanting his mother to turn everything over to him. And there are those rumors that he's been talking about selling to a competitor."

"But poisoning the best-selling product you make and blowing up people aren't going to get you a good price for the business," Laura said. She shifted to angle toward Jace. "And Parker couldn't count on his father going to the office this morning."

"Maybe he had the explosive with him and saw his chance," Jace said.

She took out her phone and pulled up Ramirez's

number. "We stopped by the hospital and spoke to Parker," she said after her colleague had answered. "He says the bomb exploded when his dad started to open his office door."

"That sounds right," Ramirez said. "The explosives expert says this was like the others, wired to go off when a door opened."

"So no timer?" Laura asked.

"No timer," Ramirez said. "And nothing to say when the bomb was put there. Donna Stroud says no one has been in her husband's office all week. After he was diagnosed with dementia and stopped working, she moved out anything that pertained to active business. She left a computer and some older files to keep him calm on the days when he did venture into the office."

"Did she say how often Steve came in to work?" Laura asked.

"Every week to ten days he would slip away from her or his minder and come down there."

"So Steve Stroud was the intended target?" Laura asked.

"It looks that way."

"What does Leo say?"

"We haven't talked to him, but we will soon."

"I've been looking into Parker's financials and I found some things you need to know," Laura said. She filled Ramirez in on the secret bank account and the possible blackmail.

"When did you find this out?" Ramirez asked.

"Last night." She felt a stab of guilt as she remembered her initial resolve to contact her fellow agent right away, a resolve that had faded as soon as she was in Jace's arms.

"Steve Stroud's death tells us this was definitely aimed at the Stroud family, not just the factory," Ramirez said. "That's the angle we'll be hitting hard going forward."

"Anything else we should know?" Laura asked.

"The girlfriend, Ms. Winger, was here causing a scene. She corralled a bunch of reporters and told them it was the FBI's fault that her fiancé was at death's door."

"She won't be the last person to say that," Laura said.

"I didn't join the Bureau because I wanted to be popular, did you?" Ramirez asked.

"No," Laura said, and ended the call.

"I caught most of that," Jace said. "Sounds like Merry was grabbing the spotlight while she could."

"If she keeps this up, everyone except Parker is going to think of her as his fiancé." Laura tucked her phone into the pocket of her jeans.

"That may be what she's hoping for," Jace said. "Where to now?"

"Let's go back to the trailer and I'll make breakfast," she said. "Let's review what we know and brainstorm." Maybe together they could figure out the right angle of approach.

"All right." He took the next left turn and headed back toward the trailer. Away from the Stroud factory, the town looked almost normal, only the occasional media van out of place in the everyday bustle downtown. This was the atmosphere Jace had grown up in, a small town where everyone knew everyone else, so different from the string of army bases, all different yet all the same, that had made up Laura's world back then.

"Why did you join the FBI?" she asked after a moment.

"I needed a job after I came out of the military and hunting down bad guys sounded interesting. Why did you join?"

"My father suggested it." She cleared her throat. "He knew someone who knew someone— next thing I knew, I had an interview."

"Was there something else you wanted to do instead?"

"I thought about going to vet school." At his look of surprise, she added, "I like animals."

"But you don't have a pet. Do you?"

"No. This job makes it tough. But I'd like to, one day." A dog would be great, though a cat might be easier, at least at first.

"If you could go back and do things over, would you become a veterinarian?" he asked.

"No. I like this work. And I'm good at it. I'm probably a better agent than I would have been a vet."

"I was intimidated about working with you, you know?"

She stared at him. "You're kidding."

"It's the truth. I checked your record. Commendation after commendation. You have future Special Agent in Charge written all over you. Next to you, I'm a total slacker."

She cleared her throat. "I wouldn't call you a slacker." She'd checked up on him, too. He'd been a key figure in a number of high-profile investigations, but he had also been reprimanded a handful of times for crossing the line and breaking the rules. At the time, she had resented him for taking short cuts. Now, part of her envied his willingness to take risks.

"You're not as uptight as I feared," he said.

There hadn't been anything uptight about her last night. She squirmed at the memory. "I believe in playing by the rules," she said. "They're there to protect everyone. But I can see there are times when intent is as important as the letter of the law." Her father would groan if he heard such rationalization. He had raised her to walk a straight line and never question authority. But she wasn't a soldier on a battlefield. She was a civilian, involved in a different kind of battle, where the enemy was rarely obvious or even visible.

Chapter Fourteen

Merry kept an eye on Laura and Jace until they had gotten into their truck and driven away. Something wasn't right about those two, the way they had just showed up in town, not knowing anybody, and now they were up in everybody's business, asking all those questions like they had a right to know the answers. She hadn't missed the way they had cozied up to Donna Stroud, either, all sympathetic and helpful. They might have fooled the old woman into trusting them, but Merry was going to be keeping an eye on them.

Most of the reporters were drifting away now. Getting their attention had been a smart move. Now everyone would know how concerned she was for Parker and his family. How close she was to them. She spotted Donna trying to slip away and picked up her pace to intercept her. "Donna, wait!" she called.

Donna turned, the blank expression in her eyes like a slap to Merry. Parker's mother didn't even recognize her. "Have you heard how Parker is doing?" she asked. "I've been so worried." Maybe she should have said something about Steve first, but no, Parker needed their concern now. She stopped beside Donna. Merry couldn't believe the woman had gone to the trouble to put on a suit before coming down to face everyone. As if her image as a businesswoman was more important than this tragedy. "I wanted to visit Parker in the hospital, but they wouldn't let me in to see him," Merry said. "Maybe you could talk to them about that."

Donna was frowning now. "Merry, isn't it?" She didn't wait for confirmation. "Parker had surgery and is going to be all right but he needs his rest. I appreciate your concern, except it would be better if you didn't visit."

"Well, of course we don't want just anyone bothering him," Merry said. "But I'm a little different, don't you think? I mean, Parker and I are practically engaged."

"But since you aren't engaged yet, we're limiting visitation to immediate family."

Who was this "we"? And who was this witch to say who her son—a grown man—could see or not see? "Parker was with me last night," she said. "I think he'd want to see me."

Donna didn't say anything, merely looked right through her. Merry glared at her. "Parker hates you," she said. "Did you know that? He's a grown man, but you treat him like he's a fourteen-year-old. He'd do a great job of managing this business, but you'd rather leave a loony old man in charge than trust your own son."

Two spots of bright pink bloomed on Donna's cheeks, against her otherwise paper-white skin. "You have no right to talk to me that way," she said. "You need to leave now."

"I'll leave," Merry said. "But you won't get rid of me that easily. When Parker and I are married, just remember—I'm the one who'll be picking out your nursing home."

She felt Donna's stare like daggers in her back as she headed across the parking lot. That woman had better watch her step. Merry could make a lot more trouble for her than she could begin to imagine.

"How is a man supposed to get some rest if people keep interrupting me?" Parker Stroud raged from his hospital bed. "I told the nurse no visitors!"

"We need to talk to you now," Ana said.

Rogers followed and shut the door behind them. "What is this about?" Jace asked.

"We know about the blackmail." Ana kept her voice low. Conversational.

Parker visibly flinched. "What did you say?"

"We know about the money you paid out to your blackmailer—$100,000 so far." She shifted on the bed to face him more directly. "Of course, that's just a drop in the bucket compared to the balance in your Steven Parker account, but at this pace, it won't be long before you're all but bankrupt."

"I... I don't know what you're talking about." But all color had drained from his face and his heart monitor beat a rapid tattoo. As good as a lie detector, Ana thought.

"You do," Rogers said. "Someone is extorting money from you. Why is that? Is it because you put that poison in the Stomach Soothers?"

Parker swallowed and regained some of his composure. "You're just making wild accusations," he said. "You can't prove anything."

"But we will," Ana said. "We'll find out who those payments were to, and we'll trace the poison, too."

"Get out of here," he ordered. "This is harassment."

Ana stood. "We'll leave. But we're going to be watching you closely. Don't do anything foolish."

BACK AT THE TRAILER, Jace made a fresh pot of coffee while Laura tore off a big piece of parchment paper from the roll in the pantry and pinned it to the pantry door, across from the kitchen table. She unearthed a couple of markers. She welcomed the opportunity to focus on the case, to prove, if only to herself, that she and Jace could still work well together even after they had become intimate. She had always been very disciplined about keeping her personal and business lives separate. The line was fuzzier with Jace, but she intended to try to keep it clear. "Sit down and let's review what we know about this case," she said.

Chuckling, Jace pulled out a chair and dropped into it. He sipped his coffee, a half smile teasing his lips.

"What's so amusing?" Laura asked.

"Like I said, you're a future Special Agent in Charge."

He probably meant that as an insult, but she refused to take it that way. "Do you want to stand up here and write?" she asked. "Because you can."

"Oh, no. You're much better at this than I am." He sipped his coffee. "It's a good idea," he added. "Let's get to it."

She uncapped the marker and turned to the paper. "Let's start with the timeline." She wrote "May 1. First victims of poisoned Stomach Soothers."

"Go back further," Jace said. "To April 29. That's when that particular lot of medication was manufactured. It was shipped the next day."

"That's good to know." She added in this information, then listed the other known deaths. "Gini Elgin died May 2," she said. "As far as we know, that's what brings Leo into the case."

"As far as we know," Jace said.

She wrote "May 6—first bombing at Stroud

Pharmaceuticals," then added in the dates of the other bombings, along with the fatalities from each.

"All the bombs were in the executive offices," Jace said. "All places Donna Stroud was most likely to have been—the door she used when she arrived early at the office, the door to her office, and the door to her husband's office."

"She said she didn't use her husband's office," Laura said.

"But I'll bet she went in there sometimes. She was more likely to do so than anyone else."

"Donna Stroud was the most likely target," Laura said. "Why?"

"With her husband incapacitated, she's in charge of the business," Jace said.

"Who stands to gain with her out of the picture?" Laura asked. "A rival?"

"Her son would take over the business if she died or couldn't continue to manage it," Jace said.

"Anyone else?"

"We'll have to find out if anyone else inherits," Jace said.

"Merry would benefit if she married Parker," Laura said.

"I don't think Parker has any intention of marrying her," Jace said. "And unless she's a lot dimmer than she looks, she knows it."

Laura studied the paper a moment. "Let's talk about the poisoning for a minute. That's the first tragedy, and maybe it triggered everything else.

Could it have been an accident? Something gone wrong in the manufacturing process? All the ingredients in the product are natural, right? Ricin is natural, too. It's from the castor bean plant. Maybe someone mistook it for something else."

"Ricin is deadly," Jace said. "It's not something people have just lying around. It certainly isn't used in anything Stroud makes. And only a few bottles of Stomach Soothers were found to be contaminated—less than a dozen. If the ricin was mistakenly used in a whole batch of product, we would have found hundreds of bottles that were contaminated."

"Which brings us back to who had the opportunity to insert the poison in those bottles, and why?"

"There were eight people on the manufacturing line the day those packages were processed." Jace ticked the names off on his fingers. "All of them are long-time employees who are still with the company. We've checked them and nothing stands out or suggests a motive for sabotage."

"Parker Stroud runs the plant and would have easy access to all parts of the manufacturing process," Laura said.

"So would his mother," Jace said. "And his father, too."

Laura frowned. "Would Steve Stroud have put ricin in those bottles of pills? Why?"

"Let's find out where he was, just to be sure,"

Jace said. "I looked up the report on the security footage for that day. It doesn't cover the whole line, but it does show that Donna and Parker Stroud were both on the production floor, along with Gini Elgin and Merry Winger."

"Merry was there? And Gini?"

"Merry brought lunch to Parker. Gini came down to talk to him."

Laura added this information to the paper, then backed up to stand beside Jace. "Parker still has the best motive and opportunity for all the crimes," she said. "Maybe he had set the bomb for his mother and his father getting there first was an accident. Trying to save his father, Parker was hurt, which tends to direct our suspicions away from him."

"I want to talk to Merry again," Jace said. "I think she knows something she isn't telling us."

"Something about Parker?" Laura asked.

"She's hiding something. I just haven't figured out what yet."

"PARKER IS HURT? Mr. Stroud dead?" Leo clutched his head and moaned. "That wasn't supposed to happen."

"What was supposed to happen, Leo?" Rogers slapped both palms on the table and leaned over the younger man. "We know you made those bombs. Another person is dead and one badly injured because of you. If you want this to stop, you have to tell us who has the other explosives, so we can stop them."

Leo moaned and rocked in his chair. Ana sat beside him. "I know you didn't mean for this to happen," she said, her voice soft.

He shook his head. "No."

"Maybe you just thought the bombs would frighten people," Ana said. "You wanted to make them listen."

His answering groan could have been a yes.

Ana put a hand on his arm. "How many bombs did you make?" she asked.

"Six." Another long moan.

Ana locked eyes with Rogers, her alarm evident. Three people had died in the first three explosions. How many more would die if three more bombs were let loose?

"Who did you give the bombs to?" Ana asked.

He shook his head. "I can't tell you."

Rogers leaned forward again, but Ana waved him away. "Why can't you tell us?" she asked.

"Because I promised." He raised his head, his face a mask of anguish. "I swore on my mother's grave."

"I think your mother would want you to help us and stop the killing," Ana said.

"Is Parker going to be all right?"

"He had to have surgery to remove some shrapnel," Rogers said. "He should recover, though he'll probably have scars the rest of his life."

Leo's lips trembled, and he struggled for control. "Parker tried to make things right after my mother died," he said. "I didn't want to listen to him, but he never stopped reaching out. We were friends in school. He never shut me out the way some people did. The way his mother did."

"How did Donna Stroud shut you out?" Ana asked.

Anger hardened his features, making him look older. "I went to see her and she refused to talk to me. She shut the door in my face."

"I'll bet that made you angry," Rogers said. "If I were in your position, I might have wanted to do something to hurt her."

Leo didn't confirm or deny this.

"You made the bombs," Rogers continued. "Six of them. Why six?"

"I only made one to begin with. It wasn't supposed to kill anyone. Just frighten them."

"So you put the first bomb at Stroud Pharmaceuticals," Rogers said. "The one that killed Lydia Green?"

"No! I wouldn't do that. I told you, I liked Lydia."

"So you made the first bomb," Rogers said. "Then you made more?"

"Leo, you didn't put those bombs at the Stroud offices, did you?" Ana asked.

"No! I didn't. I didn't have anything to do with that."

"But you know who did put them there," Ana

said. "We need to know who that person is so that we can stop them before they hurt someone else."

Leo shook his head.

Rogers leaned over Leo, his face very close, his eyes fierce. "Three bombs have exploded, Leo. Three people have died. How many more bombs are going to kill how many more people before you tell us the truth?"

"I can't tell you." He shoved back his chair and stood, Rogers and Ana rising to their feet also. "I don't want to talk anymore," Leo said. "I want to see my lawyer."

Ana and Rogers's eyes locked again. "We'll call your lawyer," Rogers said. "She'll tell you it's in your best interest to talk to us."

He led the way out of the room, as two officers entered to escort Leo back to his cell. "He's going to break," Rogers said.

"Yes," Ana agreed. "But will he tell us in time to prevent more people dying?"

MERRY LIVED IN a pale gray cottage in a neighborhood of older homes, many in the process of being renovated. Flowers crowded the beds alongside the front fence and either side of the walkway leading to the front door—ruffled hollyhocks in every shade of pink, orange daylilies like upturned bells, red and yellow and white zinnias and snapdragons filling every gap like dropped candies. "What do you two want?" Merry asked when she answered the door.

"We wanted to make sure you're okay," Laura said.

"Why wouldn't I be okay?"

"Your fiancé is in the hospital," Laura said. "Did you get to see him?"

"No." Merry stepped onto the porch and pulled the door shut behind her. "We can talk out here." She led the way into the garden. "I tried to see him and this sour-faced nurse told me only family was allowed to visit. Then I asked Donna to talk to her and she had the nerve to tell me that until Parker and I are officially engaged, I'm not family." She snapped a fading flower from one of the hollyhocks and crushed it in her hand.

"That was harsh," Jace said.

"Oh, I wasn't surprised." Merry snatched another wilting flower head and flung it into the grass. "She's as cold as they come. She's made Parker's life miserable. He's an intelligent man with lots of great ideas for the business, yet she treats him like a stupid boy."

"Merry, you're probably closer to Parker than anyone," Jace said. "Do you have any idea who might want to hurt him or his family?"

Merry stopped and looked him in the eye. "Why are you so interested?" she demanded.

"With the factory closed, we don't have jobs," Laura said. "The police and FBI aren't getting anywhere finding the person who planted those bombs, so we figure we might as well try to solve the case ourselves."

"We haven't got anything better to do," Jace said. "Maybe, being amateurs, we'll get lucky." He winked at Laura, who quickly looked away, biting the inside of her cheek to keep from laughing.

Merry returned to dead-heading spent flowers. "If you ask me, the cops ought to be taking a closer look at Donna."

"Donna Stroud?" Laura asked.

Merry nodded. "I already told you she's cold. She probably set those bombs herself to get rid of her loony husband. She had to be paying out a fortune to have people watch him while she's working."

"But what about Angela Dupree and Lydia Green?" Laura asked. "Why would she want to kill them?"

"I don't know. Maybe Angela was too needy. Maybe the cleaner found something incriminating in the trash can and was blackmailing her?"

"Do you think Parker could have set those bombs?" Laura asked. "Maybe because he resented the way his mother treated him? He wants to be in charge of the business."

"Parker?" Merry laughed. "Parker could never kill anyone. He doesn't have the nerve." She brushed her hands on the thighs of her denim shorts. "Parker likes to complain, but he doesn't have the guts to do something like that."

"Who would you say does have the guts?" Jace asked.

Merry smiled. "His mother, but you already know that. I can't think of anyone else." She faced them, hands on her hips. "Now let me ask you a question—what are you really up to?"

Laura kept her expression bland. "What do you mean? We're trying to solve this crime so we can get our jobs back."

"I mean, what are you doing in Mayville? You don't have relatives here. You didn't know anyone here before you showed up out of the blue. This isn't some garden spot everyone wants to come to. You must have had a reason."

Laura searched for a plausible answer. She was usually good at thinking on her feet but right now she was struggling.

"My family is in Hatcher, just across the border in Tennessee," Jace said. "We wanted to be close to them, but not too close. Anyway, there aren't any jobs in Hatcher. There are here."

Merry looked disappointed. "That's the truth?"

"What were you expecting, Merry?" Laura asked. "We came for the jobs. As you pointed out, there's no other reason to be here."

"You get on so well with Donna Stroud, I thought maybe you had some connection to the family."

Jace laughed. "That's rich. So, what are we, the poor relations thrilled about living in a crappy trailer and working in their factory?"

Merry smiled. "I guess it is a little silly." The smile faded. "And I guess it shows how much Donna hates me. She'd rather hire a stranger to be her son's admin than give me the job."

"Some women are very protective of their sons," Laura said. Though she felt a pinch of sympathy for Merry. She had painted a not very attractive picture of Donna Stroud.

"Let us know if you hear anything interesting and we'll do the same," Jace said. He took Laura's arm. "We'll get out of your hair now."

Arm in arm, they left the yard. When Merry and her cottage were no longer visible, Laura relaxed a little. "Do you still think she's hiding something?"

"I don't know. But we'd better let Ramirez and Rogers know they should take a closer look at Donna Stroud."

"Yeah." They hadn't considered Donna as a suspect before now because she seemed to be the person with the most to lose in all these crimes. But what if she had even more to gain?

"For what it's worth, my mom would be thrilled to know I'd taken up with you," Jace said.

The statement, or rather, the idea that he had been thinking of her in relation to his family, startled her. "Would she really? Why?"

"You're smart. Beautiful. Not afraid to get in my face when you think I screw up. My mom would appreciate all of that."

The idea was flattering, but when she considered her father's likely reaction to Jace, the fleeting satisfaction vanished. "My dad is harder to read."

"I'm betting I dealt with plenty like him in the army. Proud, strong and loyal. Also by the book and unbending. He'd hate my guts. At least until I won him over." He grinned, surprising a laugh from her. "What? You don't think I could win him over?"

She shook her head, unable to speak. Jace had won her over, and not that long ago she would have said that was impossible. "I'm not worried about my dad." She took his hand. "My dad taught me to make my own decisions, so my opinion is the only one that really counts."

"What is your opinion?" He tried to keep his voice light, but she heard the tension in his words.

"You're more complicated than I thought," she said. "I like complicated."

"We have that in common." He squeezed her hand, sending a thrill through her. She could get used to this, but she didn't trust the feeling. As an agent, she was confident in her ability to evaluate a situation and stay on top of a case. But when it came to romance, she was a rank amateur, and she didn't like her odds of succeeding.

THE FOURTH BOMB exploded at two o'clock the next morning, on Merry Winger's front porch. No one was injured, but the explosion sent a wave of terror through the town. Before, the Strouds had clearly been the target of the bomber. Now, it seemed, almost anyone could be a victim.

The poisonings had frightened people, but to avoid that danger, all you had to do was avoid taking Stomach Soothers—or all Stroud products if you were extra cautious.

But a bomb—how did you avoid a bomb? How did you live with that kind of fear?

Chapter Fifteen

"Where were you last night from approximately 8 p.m. until 6 a.m.?"

Donna Stroud, pale and disheveled, didn't look like herself without her suit and makeup. The local police had visited her home a little after seven that morning, and found her dressed in faded pink cotton trousers and a Smoky Mountains National Park T-shirt. To Ana, she scarcely resembled the competent professional she had met with her first day in town.

"Where was I last night?" Confusion clouded Donna's blue eyes. "Why is that important?"

"Please answer the question," Ana said. She and Rogers and Captain Simonson, of the Mayville Police Department, sat across the table from Donna and her lawyer, Adam Sepulveda, a local attorney who, after blustering a few feeble protests, had remained silent, occasionally fidgeting in his chair or tugging at his tie.

"I was at the hospital, visiting my son, until almost eight," Donna said. "Then I went home."

"Was anyone at home with you?" Ana asked.

"No."

"Did you talk to anyone on the phone, or speak to a neighbor? Is there anyone who can confirm that you were home last night?"

Donna sat up straighter, a little life coming back into her face. "I told you I was there and I don't lie. There isn't any other proof, but I don't see why you need it."

"What's your relationship with Merry Winger?" Rogers asked.

Donna's eyebrows rose, disappearing beneath her fringe of short bangs. "Merry works in the administrative offices of Stroud Pharmaceuticals. She is also involved with my son."

"Involved?" Ana thought this was an interesting word choice.

"I know he sleeps with her and buys her gifts, but I've rarely seen them out together, and he's never brought her to our house, so I wouldn't call her his girlfriend."

"You don't like her," Rogers said.

"She wouldn't be my first choice for my son, but most people learn best by making their own mistakes."

"You think Merry is a mistake?" Ana asked.

"Time will tell." She spread her hands flat on the table in front of her. "What is this about? Has something happened to that girl?"

"Why do you think something happened to

her?" Rogers asked. "What would have happened?"

"You asked me where I was last night. That tells me you're trying to establish my alibi. Then you ask me about Merry, a young woman I scarcely know. I don't have to be an amateur detective to put the two ideas together. Did something happen to her?"

"Merry is fine," Ana said. "But a bomb exploded on her front porch this morning."

Donna stared, mouth slack and eyes wide. She made a low sound in the back of her throat, and Ana was afraid for a moment that the older woman was having a heart attack or stroke. Ana touched her arm and Donna stared at her, then gradually came back to herself. She wet her lips. "Was it…was it like the others?" she asked.

"It was similar," Rogers said.

In fact, the bomb was identical to the other three, set to go off when the front door was opened, as Merry would have done when she went out to work in her flower garden or to get into her car, parked at the curb. Instead, the bomb had exploded when her neighbor had driven by on his way to work, in a custom pickup with oversized tires, rumbling exhaust and throbbing bass that shook the windows of every house as it passed.

"The bomb exploded accidentally," Ana said. "No one was hurt, but if Merry had opened her front door, she would have been killed, or very badly injured."

Donna covered her mouth with her hand and tears filled her eyes.

"Did you put that explosive device on Merry Winger's front porch?" Rogers asked.

"No! I would never do something like that. Not to anyone, ever!"

"My client is a law-abiding pillar of the community who has never had so much as a traffic ticket," the lawyer said. "I strongly object to this line of questioning."

"You're not in court," Rogers said. He turned his attention back to Donna. "Do you have any idea who might have put that bomb on Merry's front porch?"

"No. I swear if I did, I would tell you. I want this to stop."

"Mrs. Stroud, the first explosion at Stroud Pharmaceuticals, on May 6, was wired to a side door used only by personnel who had a key," Rogers said. "You yourself stated that you were usually the first person at the office each morning, and that you always entered via that door. Several people have confirmed this."

"Yes."

"Yet the morning the bomb exploded, you were not the first to arrive at the building. Instead, Lydia Green opened that door and was killed."

"I was dealing with my husband. He was agitated and I had to calm him down before I came to work."

"The second explosive device was wired to the door of your office," Rogers continued. When it exploded, it killed Angela Dupree. Again, you were late for work that day, something several people have stated was highly unusual."

"My husband isn't at his best in the mornings."

"The third explosion, the one that killed your husband and injured your son, was wired to your husband's office door," Rogers said. "Everyone we spoke with said that you and your husband were the only people who entered that office since your husband's retirement, but he was there only occasionally. You were the mostly likely target of that explosive device and yet once again, you escaped injury."

"What are you implying?" Donna asked.

"We've reviewed the incorporation papers for Stroud Pharmaceuticals," Ana said. "As written, your husband has primary authority over the business until his death. No provision was made in the case of his disability by illness or injury. While you were acting administrator, you had no real authority to expand or sell the business. Your ability to borrow money for the business was also limited. Your husband's death frees you to make those kind of decisions."

"I did not kill my husband," Donna said, her

voice trembling. She gripped the edge of the table. "I didn't kill anyone."

"Mrs. Stroud has lost her husband." The lawyer stood. "Her own life has been threatened several times. For you to suggest—"

"Someone connected with Stroud Pharmaceuticals is planting these bombs and killing people," Rogers said. "It's our job to take a hard look at everyone who had motive and opportunity. Mrs. Stroud had both."

"I didn't do it," Donna said. "I swear." She bent her head and began to weep, shoulders shaking.

Ana turned away. Though she wasn't convinced of Donna's innocence, she felt sorry for this woman who had lost so much.

"We can continue this interview later," Rogers said.

"I demand that you release my client at once," the lawyer said.

"She's free to go," Rogers said. "But we're continuing our investigation."

Ana walked with Rogers to the observation room where Smitty and Cantrell waited with Rowan, who had returned to Mayville last night. "How long do you think it's going to be before a story shows up in the local paper about how the FBI is bullying the newly widowed patron saint of Mayville?" Rowan asked.

Rogers dropped into the chair at the end of the table. "You tell me—how long?"

"I'd say about twenty-four hours. That lawyer had the look of someone who will hurry to get the press on his client's side."

"Then he's smarter than I gave him credit for," Rogers said. "You and I both know we're not here to win friends. And right now, Donna Stroud had the most to gain from getting rid of her husband, the chief financial officer who maybe had too tight a hold on the company purse strings, and her son's lover whom she didn't approve of."

"She also had the most to lose," Smitty said. "Her husband, her best friend, and the reputation of the business she devoted most of her adult life to."

"Do you think she's innocent?" Ana asked.

Smitty tucked her long hair behind one ear. "I'm not saying she's innocent or guilty," she said. "I just think it's good to keep all the evidence in mind, not just the parts that fit one theory."

That was vintage by-the-book Smitty. Rogers glared at her. He and Smitty had clashed more than once over her penchant for telling others how to do their jobs.

Ana shifted her gaze to Cantrell. Of all the team members, he and Smitty had locked horns the most, and she expected him to come to Rogers's defense. Instead, he leaned back in his chair, relaxed. "The trouble with this case is, every one of our suspects has just as good reasons he or she isn't responsible for these crimes as anyone else," he said.

"That just tells me we need more evidence," Rogers said. "We get the right information, we'll find the right person."

"Did the locals uncover anything useful at Merry's house?" Smitty asked.

"We gave it a good going over and didn't find anything," Chief Simonson said.

"Merry says she worked in her garden until about eight last night," Rogers said. "She went in, ate a sandwich and watched TV in her bedroom until ten thirty, then went to bed. She never heard anyone outside and she didn't see anything suspicious."

"Her bedroom is at the back of the house," Simonson said. "If she had the television on, she probably wouldn't hear anyone up front. She doesn't have a dog to alert her to a stranger's presence."

"All the other explosives have been at the Stroud plant," Ana said. "Why target Merry with this one?"

"Because someone—Donna Stroud, or maybe Parker Stroud—wants to get rid of her," Cantrell said.

"Or because the bomber thinks Merry knows something, and is afraid she'll tell," Smitty said.

"Parker was in the hospital last night," Simonson said. "He's supposed to be discharged this morning."

"What about Leo?" Rogers asked.

"He's still locked up tight. And he hasn't had any visitors or talked to anyone but his lawyer, who is still advising him not to talk to law enforcement."

"Has anyone told him about this latest bombing?" Smitty asked.

"I don't think so," the captain said.

"Tell him, and let us know his reaction," Rogers said.

The door to the conference room opened and a young woman stuck her head in. "I'm sorry to disturb you, Chief, but you're needed up front. We have a, um, situation."

"What kind of situation?" Simonson asked, already on his feet.

"Parker Stroud is up front, demanding to see you."

Ana and Rogers followed the captain down the hall to the police department lobby, where Parker Stroud looked as enraged as a man can when he's leaning on crutches and dressed in sweat pants, rubber sandals and an untucked dress shirt. When he spotted the captain, he lurched forward. "Are you out of your mind?" he shouted. "Arresting my mother? Hasn't the woman suffered enough without you digging your knife in?"

"Your mother is not under arrest," the captain

said. "She agreed to answer some questions for us and you should find her at home now."

Parker spotted Ana and Rogers. "You're behind this," he said. "You can't find anyone else to pin this on, so you go after a helpless old woman."

Ana doubted Donna would thank her son for referring to her as either helpless or old. "Gathering evidence in a case like this requires asking lots of questions," she said. "We can't afford to omit anyone who might have the answers we need."

"My mother doesn't know anything." He leaned more heavily on his crutches, his face gray beneath the scruff of beard. "And she's the person someone is obviously trying to kill."

"And you have no idea who that person might be?" Rogers asked.

"No." Parker shook his head.

"What about Merry?" Ana asked.

He frowned. "What about her?"

"A bomb exploded on her front porch early this morning," Rogers said.

"Oh God." He wiped his face with his hand. "Is she—"

"She's fine," Ana said. "She was inside when it happened. No one was hurt. You hadn't heard?"

"I was just released from the hospital. No one there said anything. Where is she now?"

"I believe she's home," the captain said. "The damage was only to the porch and the front room."

"I should probably go see her," Parker said.

"You don't sound very enthusiastic," Rogers said.

"Yeah, well, I've been trying to find a way to break things off with her."

"You don't think she'll take it well?" Ana asked.

He grimaced. "Let's put it this way—if Merry gets her hand on one of those bombs, she'll probably gladly launch it at me."

Chapter Sixteen

"What are we missing?" Laura stared at the sheets of parchment she had taped to the pantry door, each filled with the notes she and Jace had made about the case. For the last hour, they had been going over everything on those pages, searching for a clue they had previously overlooked. Lists of victims, suspects, timelines, data, and other details that might or might not help solve the crimes crowded the paper, written in Laura's neat block printing.

She stabbed a finger at Steve Stroud's name. "We should have talked to him," she said. "He accused Parker of negotiating to sell the business to a competitor. What if that was true? And he kept insisting on sneaking off to his office—maybe because he knew something shady was going on there. Now we'll never have a chance to hear what he might have told us."

"He had dementia." Jace slouched in a kitchen chair, legs stretched out in front of him, hands shoved deep in the pockets of his jeans. "We didn't question him because he wasn't a reliable witness."

"We should have tried," she said. "A mistake like that could cost us this case. It may have already cost lives." The idea that Steve might still be alive if she had acted faster or done a better job nagged at her.

"Beating yourself up over this isn't going to help." Jace stood and walked to her. "Let's give it a rest." He put his arms around her and drew her close. "Tomorrow morning we'll be fresher. Maybe we'll see something new."

She leaned against him, drawing strength from the power of his arms around her. She had always resisted the idea of dating within the Bureau, believing it wise to keep her work life and the rest of her life strictly separate. But there was something to be said for being with someone who understood how consuming the job could be, and the emotional as well as the physical toll the work could take.

He brushed his lips across her temple, then her cheek, then he found her mouth and kissed her deeply, until she was breathless, her whole body humming with desire. He danced his fingers down her bare arms, sending tremors of pleasure through her. He grasped her hips and she arched toward him, weak-kneed with wanting.

"I think we should go to bed now," he said, his

voice rough. "Though I'm tempted to take you right there on the table."

His impatience sent a fresh heat through her. She had a vision of plates and papers flying as he laid her back on the table. "Too messy," she said, breathless. "Too…hard."

"I thought you liked it hard." He rocked forward, letting her feel how ready he was for her.

She responded by cupping his fly, smiling as he hissed out a breath through his teeth. Still holding him, she started backing toward the bedroom, thrilling to the naked desire in his eyes as he followed her.

She was more sure of herself with him this time, a little more bold. After they undressed, when he took the condom from the box by the bed, she claimed the little packet, pushed him back on the mattress, and sheathed him while he watched, reaching for her when she straddled him.

They made love at a leisurely pace, watching each other as they moved, not saying much, but so intensely in the moment words hardly seemed necessary. He let her take the lead, responding to her guidance with a skill that kept her on edge for a long time before she came.

Afterward, she lay in his arms, spent and satisfied. "No more bombs tonight," he murmured, pulling the blankets over her shoulders. "I feel too good to move for at least the next eight hours."

She tried to think of a reply, but drifted to sleep before the words came to her.

Then she was in a house full of dark rooms, running from some unseen pursuer, barefoot and panicked, up steep flights of stairs and down long, narrow hallways. She stopped at the door at the end of the hallway, but it refused to open, no matter how hard she pulled on the knob or shoved at the swollen frame. Meanwhile, her pursuer came closer, his footsteps heavy on the bare wooden floors, his dark silhouette filling her with terror.

"Laura, wake up. It's all right. It's only a dream."

She came to with the sensation of landing hard on the floor, though she was safe in bed, Jace holding her to him. "It's okay." He smoothed her hair back from her face and kissed her forehead. "You're safe," he said.

"I dreamed someone was chasing me," she said. "And I couldn't get away. The door was locked and I couldn't escape."

"It doesn't take Freud to figure out that one," he said. "You're pursued by the case you can't solve." He pulled her closer. "Don't be so hard on yourself. You're doing all you can. We all are."

She nodded, but she didn't believe him. Yes, everyone on the team was working hard, but was it hard enough? Was she letting her personal life—her relationship with Jace—distract her from the job? Her father's voice echoed in her head: *Duty before self. Service to your country demands no less.* That was the life he had lived, reminding her whenever she whined about not seeing him enough that he had a whole company of soldiers who depended on him, and she was just one little girl.

"No more bad dreams," Jace said, rubbing her shoulder. "I'm here with you."

Her eyes stung, and she closed her eyes to hold back the tears, breathed in deeply his clean, masculine scent, and fell asleep in his arms, not dreaming, not afraid, not alone.

JACE WOKE AT first light and slipped out of bed without waking Laura. He went into the kitchen and started coffee, then stood at the back window and watched the sunrise filter through the trees. The world looked so peaceful this time of day. Even in the worst of the fighting in Afghanistan there had been a kind of peace at sunrise, as if everything was pausing, taking a deep breath before the next bad thing happened.

The rich aroma of coffee drifted to him and he turned to pull a mug from the cabinet. The sound of water running told him Laura was awake, and he took down a second mug for her, then smiled to himself. He had begun this assignment thinking it might be difficult to pretend to be married to her. Instead, he had fallen into the role so easily it frightened him sometimes. She was so fierce, and prickly, strong yet sensitive. He felt protective of her, though he was aware she didn't really need him at all. She wasn't his type—he liked simple women who didn't demand a lot from him. Laura was complicated, the type of woman with high standards he had no hope of meeting.

Yet here they were together, and it felt good. It felt right. He swallowed coffee, almost burning his tongue, glad of the pain to clear some of the sentimental fog from his head. Being with Laura right now was great, but he'd be a fool to think they had a future together. Sooner or later the lust would wear off and they'd go back to being two people with different ways of looking at the world.

Laura shuffled into the kitchen, damp hair curling around her face. "Good morning," he said, and filled a mug with coffee and handed it to her.

"Thanks." She closed her eyes and drank deeply, then sighed. "I've been thinking about the case," she said.

And here I was hoping you were thinking about me. But he didn't say it—the words were too close to the truth. "Did you come up with any new angles?" he asked instead.

"Whoever Leo made those bombs for, it's someone who knew he had the ability to make them," she said. "Someone he cares enough about to risk breaking the law for. Someone he won't give up, even to save himself."

Leo didn't have siblings or children of his own. "A lover?" Jace asked.

"I think so." Laura sipped more coffee.

"Man or woman?" Jace asked.

"It could be either," she said. "We need to dig deeper."

"He's not that old," Jace said. "I can't think he would have had that many serious relationships."

"We should start with high school," she said. "He went to school here in town and sometimes young relationships are extra intense. Maybe he reconnected when he came back here following his mother's death. His old flame saw the chance to even some scores with the Strouds."

"You're thinking someone who works at the plant?" Jace asked. "All the evidence points that way."

"Right. So we go to the school, ask questions, check the yearbook. He was the mad bomber, so he has that reputation to build on, even if the bomb he made back then wasn't real." She set her cup aside and straightened. "It's your turn to make breakfast while I get dressed. Then we can visit the high school."

And that was that. No good morning kiss. Nothing about last night. The ardent lover of last night replaced by all-business Special Agent Smith.

Complicated.

MAYVILLE HIGH SCHOOL—Home of the Mayville
Wild Cats!—had the institutional appearance
shared by schools and prisons, the former usually with a large sports complex nearby, the latter
encircled with razor wire. On this late-spring Saturday, the campus was nearly deserted, and their
steps echoed as they crossed the empty parking
lot to the front entrance.

"Were you a jock in high school?" Laura asked.
"Quarterback of the football team, basketball
star?"

"Tight end," he said. "And I played baseball,
not basketball. Pitcher." In those days, he had
dreamed of going pro, but he'd never had that
kind of talent. "Let me guess, you were valedic-
torian."

She stared. "How did you know?"

"How could you not be?" He held open the
door to the front office. Principal Mike Caldwell
had agreed to meet them here.

The burly man with the gray crew cut who
emerged from a back office to greet them reminded Jace of every drill sergeant he had ever
met. Caldwell shook both their hands, examined
their IDs, then ushered them into his office. "I'm
guessing this has something to do with that mess
over at Stroud," he said, settling his big frame
behind a desk almost obscured by neat stacks of
papers. "How can I help?"

"We're trying to find out more about a former student," Laura said. "Leo Elgin."

"I heard you'd arrested him. I suppose you heard about that whole mad bomber fiasco. It wasn't a real bomb, just a hotheaded kid being stupid."

"Did you know Leo?" Laura asked.

"Oh, I knew him. I coached football and track and taught civics. I had Leo in one of my classes."

"What was he like?" Jace asked. "Other than hotheaded."

"He was smart. Too smart for his own good. What I mean is kids like that get bored, then they get into trouble, like that fake bomb thing." He leaned forward, hands clasped on the desk. "Leo had a beef with the teacher he'd given the thing to. She'd marked him down on an exam for getting an answer wrong. Something to do with a higher mathematical theory. Turns out, Leo was right and she was wrong, but he never forgave her for the mistake."

"So he held grudges?" Laura asked.

"Yes, I'd say so."

"Was he popular?" Jace asked. "Who were his friends?"

"He was popular enough. Not in the most popular crowd, but most people seemed to like him. He had a reputation as a kind of a rebel and some kids admire that."

"Any girlfriends?" Jace asked.

Caldwell nodded. "He was surprisingly popular with the girls. I don't remember him being involved with anyone in particular, but he had quite a few female admirers, considering he wasn't athletic or all that good-looking."

"Can you think of anyone he dated who still lives in the area?" Jace asked. "Anyone who works at Stroud?"

Caldwell rubbed his chin. "I can't, really," he said.

"Do you have yearbooks from when Leo was a student here?" Laura asked. "We'd like to look at them."

"I do." He rolled his chair to the bookcase that filled most of the back wall, selected four thick volumes, then rolled over to the desk and slid them to Laura.

"The Beacon," Jace read the name on the cover of the top volume.

Caldwell stood. "I've got to attend a graduation rehearsal this afternoon, but you're welcome to use my office to look at those."

"Thanks," Jace said. "But we might want to take one or more of them with us."

"Just promise to return them, please. We have a complete set dating back to 1926 and I'd hate to break up the collection."

"Sure thing. We'll give you a receipt."

Laura was already engrossed in the first volume by the time Jace pulled the truck into the driveway of the trailer. "The index has a list of every student by class," she said. "Start there and see how many names ring a bell. Later, we can compare them with the employee list from Stroud."

In the next hour they found the names of a dozen former students who now worked at Stroud, including Parker Stroud. They looked at Leo's picture. He stared into the camera directly, an approximation of a sneer curling his lip. "Tell me the truth," Jace said. "Would he have done it for you when you were a high school girl?"

She shrugged. "Hard to say. I liked smart guys. And there's something about a bad boy." Laughter danced in her eyes and he fought the urge to lean over and kiss her.

Instead, he shut the book. "There are pictures in here of Leo with groups of kids, but nothing that says 'big romance' to me."

"To me, either." She studied the stack of books and shook her head. "I don't think there's anything here. We need to try college."

"He attended West Virginia University," Jace said. "That's about three hours from here."

Laura shoved back her chair and rose. "Then it's time for a road trip."

Chapter Seventeen

Merry logged on to her online bank account Saturday morning and smiled to herself when she saw the balance. Parker was so generous. Too bad things weren't going to work out the way she had hoped. But a smart woman knew when to cut her losses.

She signed out of the bank's website and clicked over to the travel page she had bookmarked. Where should she take her dream vacation?

Her phone rang. Annoyed at the interruption, she checked the display. Why was Donna Stroud calling her? Maybe all the bad press had guilted the Strouds into offering to pay the employees who'd been put out of work by the sudden plant closure. It wasn't like the family couldn't afford it. "Hello?" Merry injected an extra note of pleasantness into her voice.

"Merry, it's Donna Stroud."

Had the woman never heard of caller ID? "Hello, Mrs. Stroud. How are you doing?"

"I'm as well as can be expected. I called because I've decided to operate Stroud Pharmaceuticals out of my home office until the plant reopens. I'll need you to report there for work at nine Monday morning. You know where that is, don't you?"

Did she know where that was—really! The Strouds only owned the biggest house in town, a white-columned monstrosity straight out of *Gone with the Wind*. "I can't come in Monday," Merry said.

"Why not?" Donna asked.

"I have two weeks' time off due. While the plant is closed, I decided to take a vacation."

"I really need you to put that on hold until this situation is resolved," Donna said. "I know it's a sacrifice, but it's necessary for the future health of the company."

Merry didn't give a fig about the company. "I'm sorry, but I've already booked my tickets." She hit the Purchase Reservation button.

"How long will you be gone?" Donna asked.

"I'm not sure." She had purchased a one-way ticket.

"Merry, I can't allow this," Donna said. "You should have talked to me before you made your plans."

"Excuse me, but you're not my mother. I don't need your permission to take a vacation."

"There's no need to take that attitude. I'm sim-

ply saying I expect every team member to contribute one-hundred percent during this crisis."

"Then I guess I'm no longer a part of the team."
Elation surged through her. She only wished she
could see Donna's face.

"What did you say?" Donna asked.

"I said I quit. I'm going on vacation." She
ended the call and tossed the phone on the desk.
Then she hit Print and turned to collect the reservation confirmation from the printer behind her.
A one-way ticket to Brazil.

She had always wanted to see Rio.

THE SECURITY FIRM Donna Stroud had hired to patrol the closed campus of Stroud Pharmaceuticals
hesitated only a moment when Merry presented
them with a letter on Donna Stroud's personal
stationery, authorizing Merry Winger to access
the executive offices for the purpose of retriev-
ing some important documents. "This won't take
long," Merry reassured the guard when he told
her she could go on in. She already had all the
papers she needed. This visit was merely so the
guard would remember her and verify she had
indeed been there.

She unlocked the door and went first to the executive offices. She rifled through all the desks
scoring about forty dollars in miscellaneous coins
and bills and a hidden stash of pain pills—you
never knew when those might come in handy.

In Donna Stroud's desk she found a file conveniently labeled FBI. Curious, she flipped through it, a thrill rushing through her as she found the employment paperwork for Laura Lovejoy—real name, Laura Smith. Or rather, Special Agent Laura Smith.

Parker's new admin was a spy! So, apparently, was her husband, whose name wasn't Lovejoy either, but Jason Cantrell. Now wasn't that interesting?

Merry returned the file to the drawer, spent a few more minutes in Donna's office, then hurried down the hall to Parker's office.

She felt under Parker's center desk drawer and found the little lever that released the catch on a second, thinner drawer. She already had a copy of the bank book inside the drawer, but why not retrieve the original, as long as she was here? She smiled at the small black book, and at Parker's fondness for paper trails. She slid the book into her purse, then left the office with only a small pang of regret. She would have enjoyed being Mrs. Parker Stroud. Parker wasn't bad-looking, was a decent lover, and his money and name would have eased any dissatisfaction she might have experienced down the road. But maybe she was destined for better things.

She waved to the guard and drove out of the lot, then picked up her phone and hit the button to dial the number she had already typed in. "Hello?" Laura Lovejoy sounded annoyed.

"I need to see you right away," Merry said. "It's really important."

"We're on our way out of town," Laura said. "Maybe later—"

"Not later. Now." Merry was the one calling the shots here. "I've found out something important about Parker that the FBI needs to know."

"Then why are you calling me?" Laura asked.

"Because I know who you are, Agent Smith. And we need to talk now."

"Fine." The word was clipped. Impatient. "Where do you want to meet?"

"I'll come to you. Don't worry, I know the address."

Ten minutes later, she turned onto the rutted dirt road that led to the single-wide trailer set back under the trees. Jace and Laura stood on the porch and watched Merry climb out of her car. "The feds couldn't find any better place to put you up than this dump?" Merry asked as she made her way up the graveled path that led to the bottom of the steps.

Jace opened the front door wider. "Come in, Merry."

"How did you find out our identities?" Laura asked as she followed Merry into the living room.

"Because I'm smart." She sat in the recliner and looked up at them. They took up positions on either end of the sofa. "Are you two really married, or is that part of the play-acting, too?" Merry asked.

"What did you want to talk to us about?" Jace asked.

She reached for her purse and both agents tensed. "Don't worry, I'm not pulling a gun," Merry said. She took out the bank book and tossed it to Laura. "Take a look at that."

Laura flipped through the book, then handed it to Jace. "Where did you get that?"

"I found it in Parker's desk," Merry said. "Just now, when I went to pick up some papers for Mrs. Stroud." If they bothered to check with Donna, the old woman would deny sending Merry on such an errand, but Merry was counting on the cops to be so anxious to get their hands on Parker, they wouldn't bother to check her story until she was long gone to Rio.

"Thank you for bringing this to us," Laura said. "We'll certainly look into it."

She didn't even act surprised. Which meant the FBI already knew about Parker's secret account. Disappointing. But all wasn't lost. "Don't you want to know what it means?"

"What do you think it means?" Jace asked.

Merry adopted a sad face. Sad, and a little terrified. "I think Parker is the one who poisoned the Stomach Soothers. Looking back, it all makes sense now."

Another exchange of looks between the two. "Tell us what you know," Jace said.

She bit her lip, as if reluctant to get Parker—the man she loved—into trouble. Then she nodded. She had to do the right thing, even if it cost her her future happiness. "I think Parker was embezzling money from his family's company," she said. "He put the proceeds into that secret account. But Gini Elgin, the chief financial officer, must have noticed something was off. I overheard her confronting him on the factory floor one day. I caught the words 'the money isn't right.' That night, Parker was so furious. He wouldn't tell me why, but he did say that Gini was poking her nose where it didn't belong. The next day, I caught him in the herb garden."

"The herb garden?" Laura was wearing her annoyed look again. Merry wanted to laugh.

"It's a garden in front of the Stroud plant, with examples of all the plants Evangeline Stroud, the company founder, used in her original herbal remedies. There are paths and a gazebo and little markers identifying everything. I helped with some of the plantings, since I have a green thumb."

"What was the significance of Parker being in the garden?" Jace asked.

"First of all, he never went there," Merry said. "He used to tease me about my interest in gardening. But he was there that day, so I paid closer attention, to see what he was doing. That's when I noticed he was standing right next to the castor plant. You know about castor plants, right?"

"Ricin is derived from castor beans," Laura said.

Merry nodded. "That didn't register with me until much later, but I think now he poisoned those tablets in order to kill Gini without anyone suspecting him. As plant manager, he had plenty of opportunity to slip the poison into the pills and substitute that bottle for the one she always kept in her desk. Everyone knew she took the Stomach Soothers all the time."

"This is really important," Jace said. "Do you know if Parker has any more ricin? Or more contaminated pills?"

Why hadn't she thought of this? The idea scared her a little. "I don't know," she said. "I haven't seen any in his home or office."

"When did you start blackmailing him?" Jace asked, just as smooth as if he'd been asking how she took her coffee.

But Merry didn't even blink. "Blackmail?" she asked.

"You went to Parker, told him what you knew, and he paid you $50,000 a week," Laura said.

Merry laughed. "I wish. But seriously, I didn't need to blackmail Parker. We were going to get married. He's so generous, buying me anything

I want, and everything he had was going to be mine."

"You're using the past tense," Jace said. "Is the wedding off?"

Tears stung her eyes. She was really good at this acting stuff, wasn't she? "I can't marry a man who murdered six people," she said. "I love Parker, but he needs help. And what if my life is in danger because I told you?" She jumped up and turned as if to leave.

Jace took her arm. Not roughly, but there was muscle behind his grip. "Calm down," he said. "Sit down and tell us what you know about the bombs."

She sat, taking the opportunity to regroup. "I don't know anything about the bombs," she said.

"Do you think Parker set them?" Laura asked.

"I don't know what to think." She stared at her lap, then lifted her head to meet Laura's gaze. "I would have said Parker would never do something like that, but he and Leo have been friends for years, and then when that bomb exploded at my house…"

"You thought Parker was trying to kill you?" Jace asked.

"I thought maybe he saw me the day he was in the garden, and he was afraid I'd tell someone." She buried her face in her hands. "Now I'm terrified. You have to do something." This time when she stood, no one tried to stop her.

"We can take you into protective custody," Laura said. "Keep you safe."

"No. I don't want that!" She softened her voice. "I'll be okay. Just keep me posted, okay?" She paused at the door. "And I promise not to tell anybody you're agents," she said.

"We will be in touch." Laura put her hand over Merry's on the doorknob. "We'll be checking and if we find out you blackmailed Parker, we will arrest you."

Merry glared, then shoved past Laura and out the door. Let them look. Parker wasn't the only one with a secret account, and even if the feds found that bank, Merry had already moved the funds to an even more secure location. Tomorrow she'd be on her way to Brazil, out of their reach forever.

Chapter Eighteen

Sunday morning, Laura felt more like herself again, dressed in her own clothes. She patted her chignon, every hair in place, and buttoned the middle button of her suit jacket, then went to meet Jace in the living room of the trailer. With luck, by this time tomorrow they'd both be back in their own apartments in Knoxville.

Jace had donned a suit for this occasion as well, though he had yet to put on the jacket. His gaze swept over her as she entered the room, and she wondered if he was comparing her current look to the clothing she had worn while posing as a struggling newlywed.

Or maybe he was just remembering how she looked naked.

"Are you ready to do this?" he asked.

"I've been looking forward to it."

Driving to arrest someone in a beat-up mustard-colored pickup didn't have the same panache as arriving in a black sedan, but at least Parker

Stroud wouldn't be overly alarmed when he saw them pull up to his house.

The two police cruisers and Ramirez and Rogers's sedan might set off a few alarm bells, of course, but, since they would have the house surrounded, Laura wasn't expecting Parker to give them much trouble.

As it was, they had to wait on the front steps of his house for several minutes and ring the bell three times before Parker, hobbling on crutches, answered the door. "What are you doing here?" he demanded, scowling.

Laura opened the folder with her credentials and held them at eye level. "Parker Stroud, I'm arresting you for the murders of Virginia Elgin, Herbert Baker, Gail Benito..." She read off all the names of the people who had died after ingesting the tainted Stomach Soothers. She might have added the names of those who had died in the bombings—including Parker's own father— but the team was still building that case.

As she spoke, Parker's jaw went slack and all color drained from his face. When she had finished reciting the charges, Jace stepped forward. "Turn around and put your hands behind your back," he said, relieving Parker of his crutches and steadying him as he did so.

"There must be some mistake." Parker's voice was thin and reedy, more frightened boy than murderous man.

"Turn around, Mr. Stroud." Jace continued to steady him, alert for any attempt to fight back.

He turned, but looked back at Laura as Jace cuffed him. "I want my lawyer," he said.

"You can contact him when we get to the station." Local police would process and hold Parker until he could be transported to a federal facility. "You have the right to remain silent…"

She recited the Miranda warning, but she doubted if much was registering. Two police cars, along with Ramirez and Rogers, had arrived before Parker snapped out of his daze. "Hey!" he called as Laura was moving away, having handed him over to two officers for transport to the station. "What are you doing arresting me? You're my secretary."

"I have a lot of talents," she said, and walked back to the truck.

Jace fell into step beside her. "That's you," he said. "Multitalented." Somehow, he managed to imbue the words with a sexy heat that melted a few synapses. She shot him a stern look, which he met with a wicked grin that turned up the heat another notch.

While the local cops processed Parker, Laura and Ramirez joined Rogers in searching Parker's home. The four-bedroom, five-bath home featured a media room, billiard table, walk-in closets, and a pool and spa. One of the bedrooms was being used as a home office and they started the search there, donning gloves and methodically combing through every drawer, opening every book, and feeling behind every painting.

Laura found the flash drive, tucked in the toe of a pair of dress shoes at the back of the master bedroom closet. She connected it to the laptop from the office and smiled as rows of figures populated the screen.

"What are we looking at?" Jace leaned over her shoulder and studied the images.

"I'm pretty sure these are the missing financials from Stroud Pharmaceuticals," she said. She pointed to a column of red figures. "These are all the places the income and expenses don't match up. My guess is Gini Elgin spotted these and connected the missing money to Parker. That's probably what they were arguing about that day on the factory floor, and why he decided to kill her."

"Why keep these files?" he asked. "Why not destroy them?"

"Sooner or later, the company would be due for an audit. Missing data gets flagged and that would be a real problem. So I think he planned to use this file as a basis for reconstructing the data to paint a more favorable financial picture. Especially if he planned to partner with a competitor, or even sell the business outright."

"Steve Stroud was telling the truth," Jace said. "Even if no one believed him."

"Maybe that's why Parker planted that bomb

in his dad's office," she said. "He couldn't risk someone—like the FBI—finally paying attention to Steve."

"He took a big risk, following his father into the building," Jace said.

"Maybe he thought doing so would remove suspicion from him." Laura removed the drive from the computer and slipped it into an evidence bag. "It almost worked."

Ramirez and Rogers joined them in the office. "We've been through the whole house," Rogers said. "No medication, though we found a container of castor beans in the back of the pantry."

"We'll get a team out here tomorrow to start looking in the walls and floors," Ramirez said. "Let's go talk to Parker and see what he has to say for himself."

PARKER REMINDED JACE of a life-sized balloon figure that had sprung a leak. Everything about him sagged, from his shoulders to his face. He didn't even look up when Jace and Laura entered the room. They had decided they would question him first, and depending on the progress they made, Ramirez and Rogers would follow up.

A handsome older man with a luxurious white moustache stood to greet the two agents and introduced himself as Gerald Kirkbaum. "I commend you on your dedication to finding the person responsible for these tragic deaths," he said. "But there's been some terrible mistake. Mr. Stroud had nothing to do with those deaths. He had no reason to do such a horrible thing."

Parker didn't look innocent to Jace. In fact, he had never seen anyone who looked guiltier. "We think he did have a reason," Laura said.

She pulled out a chair and sat. Parker still hadn't looked at her. Mr. Kirkbaum remained standing, as did Jace. "You have no evidence—" Kirkbaum began.

"We have evidence," Laura said, speaking to Parker. "We have a witness who presented us with a bank book, showing the secret account where you've been stashing the money you embezzled from Stroud Pharmaceuticals." She leaned toward him, addressing the top of his bowed head. "This same witness saw you arguing with Gini Elgin when she confronted you about the missing money. And she will testify that she saw you in the garden with the castor bean plants. Castor beans are the source of ricin. But you know that, don't you? We found the castor beans in your pantry."

"Merry is a liar," he said, still not raising his head. "She's upset because I won't marry her, so she told these lies."

"I've seen the financials, and the bank account, and the castor beans," Laura said. "She isn't lying." She leaned toward him, lowering her voice. "How much did you pay Leo Elgin for those bombs? Did you think if you killed your mother and father you'd finally inherit the family business? You could run it the way you saw fit, even sell it if you liked? After all, you'd already killed six people. What were a few more? And hey, your dad was already half-gone, so what did it matter if you killed him?"

"I had nothing to do with that!" Parker's head came up and he straightened, like a puppet come to life.

Jace stepped forward. "Tell us where the other bombs are," he said. "How many did Leo make for you? Six? Or more?"

"No. I had nothing to do with that."

"I've met some heartless people in this job," Jace said. "But a man who would kill his own father, and try to kill his mother—that's lower than low."

"I didn't do it!" His shout echoed in the small room.

"We need to stop this questioning now," Kirkbaum said. "Parker, don't say another word."

But Parker was weeping, tears streaming down his face. He held out his cuffed hands to Laura, pleading. "I only meant to kill Gini. I didn't want to, but she'd found out about the money and threatened to tell my mother. I couldn't let them find out. My dad had already retired and I thought if I kept working on my mother, she'd eventually relent and turn everything over to me. Then no one would have to know."

"You're saying you put the ricin in the Stomach Soother tablets for the purpose of killing Virginia Elgin?" Jace said.

"Yes." The words were barely audible since Parker had buried his head in his hands.

"Parker, you need to shut up now." Kirkbaum leaned over his client. "You're not helping yourself."

"I didn't kill my father," Parker said, raising his head again. "And I didn't try to kill my mother. I never bought any bombs from Leo."

"Tell us more about the ricin," Laura said. "How did you know how to make it?"

"I looked on the internet," he said. "I knew about the castor bean plant because Merry had pointed it out to me. She was really into gardening and knew a lot about plants. I liked that I could make the poison myself, without having to buy anything that might be traced. I had to be careful, but it wasn't really that hard."

"How many bottles did you put the ricin in?" Jace asked.

"A whole tray. Twelve. It was the quickest way, slipping it in as they passed the filler mechanism. I went in one night after everything shut down and ran the machinery myself. I shut off all the security cameras. Then I took the whole lot out before it reached shipping." He frowned. "But I must have missed a few bottles that got slipped into the distribution stream. I put one of the bottles in Gini's desk, to replace the bottle she always kept there. But the next thing I know, all these other people were dying." He covered his face with his hands. "I never meant for that to happen."

Parker was probably hoping they would feel as sorry for him as he felt for himself, but all Jace's compassion was reserved for the six people the man had murdered. "What did you do with the rest of the bottles you pulled off the line?" he asked.

"I buried them."

"Where did you bury them?" Laura asked.

"In my mother's backyard. By the barbecue pit. I didn't know what else to do."

Jace glanced toward the observation window. Ramirez or Rogers would send someone to the Stroud home to collect that dangerous buried treasure pronto.

"When did Merry find out about what you'd done?" Laura asked.

"She saw me in the garden at the plant that day, and she saw me arguing with Gini before that. I guess after she heard how Gini died, she put everything together."

"She was blackmailing you," Laura said.

Parker nodded. "She came to me a couple of days after Gini died."

"She wanted $50,000?" Laura asked.

"That's the thing. She didn't ask for the money

at first. She said if we got married right away, she wouldn't be able to testify against me."

No one bothered to point out that this wasn't how spousal privilege worked. "But you didn't marry her," Jace said.

"I couldn't. My parents would have stroked out at the idea. There was no way my mom would have turned over the business to me if I even got engaged to Merry. And I had to get control of the business. So I made a deal to pay her the $50,000 a week and I'd marry her as soon as my mom signed the paperwork to put me in charge."

"How did she react to that?" Laura asked.

"She didn't like it, but I persuaded her it was the only way. She really wanted to be Mrs. Parker Stroud."

"She loved you that much?" Jace tried to keep the doubt from his voice.

"She didn't love me as much as she loved the idea of living in a big house and having everyone in town and most of the state fall over themselves to be her best friend. Or at least, that's how she saw it. I tried to tell her it wouldn't be like that, but she wouldn't listen."

"So Merry knew what you had done, at least since two days after Gini Elgin died," Laura said. "But she told us she didn't figure it out until a few days ago."

"If you know about my bank account, then you saw the payments I made to her," Parker said. "I made the first one on the fourth."

That matched up with the entries in the bank register Merry had given them. "Why did Merry lie to us?" Laura asked. "Did the two of you have an argument?"

"She was getting impatient. She told me I needed to stand up to my mother and insist on taking over the business and marrying her. I tried to tell her that my father had just died—this wasn't the right time, but she wouldn't listen. She said she had waited long enough. But I never thought she'd turn me in."

Laura leaned toward him. "So your agreement with Merry was that when you got control of Stroud Pharmaceuticals, you'd marry her."

"Yes."

"If your parents died, you would inherit the business," Laura said.

"I don't care what kind of monster you think I am, but I wouldn't do that." Parker's voice rose. "What do I have to do to get you to believe me?"

"I believe you," Laura said. "But if Merry thought your parents' deaths would get her what she wanted, do you think she'd try to hurry things along?"

Jace recognized the fear that blossomed in Parker's eyes. The handcuffed man opened his mouth as if to protest, but no words came out. "She asked me about Leo one day, not long after she figured out what I'd done with the Stomach Soothers," Parker said. "I told her the mad bomber story." He wet his lips. "I didn't think anything of it, but then later, Leo told me Merry had been to see him. He said she'd been really nice and asked about his job, and agreed with him that the Strouds—my mom and dad—were as good as murderers."

"When did he tell you that?" Jace asked.

"We met at the lake one evening, a few days before his mother's funeral. I'd heard what he was saying around town—that my family had killed his mother. I tried to talk some sense to him, but he wouldn't listen."

"What about the money you paid him?" Laura asked.

"It really was for the funeral." He looked pained. "But Merry volunteered to deliver it to him. She said Leo would take it better coming from her, that the two of them were friends now, because they both knew what it was like to get a raw deal from the Strouds."

"That's pretty harsh," Jace said.

"She could say anything she wanted to me now and I couldn't do anything about it."

Laura's chair scraped back and she stood. "That's all the questions we have for now."

She left the room, Jace on her heels. "We need to find Merry," she said as they hurried down the hall.

"You think she planted those bombs," Jace said.

"Yes, and you saw those notes she sent to Donna. She isn't finished yet."

Chapter Nineteen

Merry hefted the second of two large suitcases into the trunk of her car, then slammed the lid. She had spent too much time packing, but it had been hard to decide what to take. She would be gone a long time, and she wasn't sure what she'd need. In the end, she'd consoled herself with the knowledge that she had enough money to buy new things. And what she did have was bound to go farther in South America, right?

Besides, she had a lot more money now. The cops—and eventually Parker—would think she'd just stolen Parker's passbook to turn over to the police, but she'd also taken his passwords, and even the answers to his secret questions that were part of account security. With that information, she'd been able to transfer most of the $10 million balance into her own account. It had been so easy. And with that kind of money, who needed the Strouds? They were nobodies.

She slid into the driver's seat and drove toward town. She had one quick stop before she headed to the airport. In the oppressive afternoon heat, the trailer looked even shabbier than she remembered, the heart-shaped catalpa leaves drooping.

She parked in the shade of that tree and hurried up the walk. The cheap lock popped with one thrust of her credit card between the door and the jamb, and Merry was in and out in less than five minutes. Then again, she'd had a lot of practice delivering her little gifts.

Humming to herself, she pressed down on the gas, the speedometer climbing as she rushed toward the airport.

"She's not here," Laura said as Jace pulled into Merry's driveway. "Her car isn't out front."

"Maybe she has parking in the back," Jace said. He doubted it, but it didn't pay to overlook any possibility.

"I hope you're right." Laura shoved open the door of the truck and raced up the drive, Jace at her heels. She pounded on the front door. "Merry! It's Laura. I need to talk to you. It's an emergency."

No answer. Jace pressed his ear to the door. No sounds of movement inside. He stepped back.

"You need to break the door down."

"Without a warrant?" He feigned shock.

She scowled at him. He stepped back, then aimed a powerful kick at the door, just above the knob. The wood splintered. Another hard kick and it sagged inward. He drew his weapon, and then they went in. "FBI!" he shouted.

The only answer was the low hum of the air conditioning.

"I'll take the bedroom. You search the rest of the house," Laura said.

"I love it when you're bossy," he called after her.

A search of the living room revealed no Merry, but in the dining room, a piece of white paper taped to the table caught his attention.

ALL THAT'S LEFT ARE TWO. GUESS WHO?

Laura appeared in the doorway to the dining room. "She's gone," she said. "There are too many empty hangers in her closet, and there's no makeup or shampoo in the bathroom."

"She left a note." Jace gestured to the table.

Laura glanced at the note, then headed for the door. "I'll call the team while you drive. The local police can put out an APB in case she's driving somewhere."

Jace finished the thought. "Meanwhile, we've got to drive to the airport."

MERRY PULLED INTO the valet lane for airport parking. No more economy lot for her. She handed the attendant her key, flagged down a red cap to take her luggage and gave him the name of her airline. She bypassed the waiting crowd and strolled to the first class desk. "Enjoy your flight, Ms. Winger," the agent said.

Yes! She could definitely get used to service like this.

She glanced around as she made her way to the security checkpoint. No one paid any attention to her. She'd taken a chance, leaving that note, but she figured Laura and her fellow feds would be busy with Parker for the next little while.

The dumb sap. He'd been stupid to think he could get away with poisoning people in the first place, and then he had made things worse by trying to play her. If he had only married her when she asked him to, she would have taken care of everything. Instead, he'd almost gotten himself blown up—twice—and now he was going to jail for the rest of his life.

She reached her gate just as the agent was calling for first class passengers. She handed over her boarding pass and walked down the Jetway to her comfortable seat. Moments later, she was sipping a glass of champagne and contemplating the future. She'd do some shopping tomorrow—buy a new bikini, or several, and clothes more suitable for the tropics. Then she'd visit a real estate agent and look into renting a nice villa. One in a good neighborhood, with security.

She only regretted she couldn't stay in Mayville to hear about the last two bombs. Leo had balked at making six for her at first, but she had promised to find the person who had killed his mother and make them pay. That, and the promise of mind-blowing sex, had persuaded him. She had never intended to deliver on the sex, but he didn't know that.

Then she had sworn to find him and castrate him if he ever told a soul about her. She had made sure he believed her, too.

Men. They were so easy to manipulate.

The last few passengers filed on and the flight attendants began closing overhead bins and readying for takeoff. Merry leaned back and closed her eyes, some of the tension that had been building these last few weeks easing away. This time tomorrow she'd be sipping a cool drink in the hot sun, planning the rest of a life of luxury.

"I'VE GOT A list of all the flights leaving from Yeager Airport in the next three hours," Laura said as Jace pulled into the valet lane for airport parking. "We're lucky this isn't a bigger airport."

"How many flights?" Jace asked as he handed the attendant his keys.

"Five."

Jace pulled up Merry's picture on his phone and showed it to the attendant. "Has this woman been through here in the last hour or so?" he asked.

The young man studied the photo, then shook his head. "I haven't seen her."

Jace turned as a second man approached. "Have you seen her?" he asked.

The second man's eyes widened. "Yeah, she was just here—maybe half an hour ago."

"What was she driving?" Laura asked.

"A white Chevy sedan."

"Thanks." Jace and Laura sprinted into the terminal.

"You take the desks on the right, I'll take the left," Laura said as they reached the check-in level.

Passengers grumbled as Jace cut to the front of the line at the first desk, but his badge silenced the agent's rebuke. "Merry Winger," he said. "Has she checked in here? She may have been using another name, but she looks like this." He showed the picture.

He struck out at the first two desks, but at the third, the agent verified that Merry Winger had checked in forty minutes before, using a one-way ticket with a final destination of Rio de Janeiro.

Jace texted Laura and headed to security. She met him there and they badged their way to the gate. An air marshal, alerted by TSA, met them. "The plane has already pulled away from the Jetway," the marshal said.

"Then they need to come back," Laura said.

"And don't let her know why the plane is returning," Jace said. "She's already killed at least three people. There's no telling what she'll do if she's cornered."

"Understood," the marshal said. "We'll do what we can to make this seem routine."

MERRY OPENED HER eyes as the speaker overhead crackled to life. "Folks, this is the captain speaking. We've got to return to the gate for a moment. No need for alarm, just a routine precaution. We promise to have you all on your way as quickly as possible."

Merry's stomach fluttered. She flagged down the flight attendant. "Why are we returning to the gate?" she asked. "I have a connection to make in Charlotte."

"You shouldn't have any trouble with your connection," she said. "The pilot is telling us this is only a quick stop."

"But why?" Merry asked, anxiety building. "We were already on the runway. They can't just make us go back."

"It happens." The flight attendant shrugged. "Try not to stress. Would you like another glass of champagne?"

Merry had just accepted the champagne when the flight reached the terminal. But instead of parking at a gate, the plane stopped away from the gates. "What's happening?" Merry asked, trying to see across the aisle and out the window that faced the terminal.

"They're bringing out one of those rolling stairs," a man across the aisle said.

"I bet they're boarding some bigwig who was late for the flight," another man said.

"Maybe it's a celebrity," a woman suggested.

"It's two people," the first man said, craning to see out the window. "Nobody I recognize, though."

Two people. Merry unbuckled her seat belt and scanned the aisle, searching for some avenue of escape. She didn't know for sure that the two people were FBI agents or police, but she wanted to be prepared, just in case.

She stood and the flight attendant hurried to her. "You need to remain in your seat, with your seat belt fastened," the attendant said.

Merry offered an apologetic smile. "I really need to use the ladies' room," she said. "All that champagne."

"I'm sorry, but you'll have to wait a few minutes more." The flight attendant blocked the aisle, refusing to let Merry move past.

Behind her, the exit door swung open. Laura entered first, followed by Jace. "Hello, Merry," Laura said.

Merry shoved the flight attendant aside. Someone screamed as Merry raced past, through the curtain separating first class from economy. "Stop that woman!" Jace shouted.

A man stood in the aisle, but Merry plowed past him, sending him staggering back into the lap of a woman seated beside the aisle.

Someone else grabbed her arm and refused to let go. She jammed her elbow into his jaw, but still he wouldn't release her. She turned to hit him again, then Laura tackled her, taking her to the floor. Strong arms dragged Merry's hands behind her back and cuffed her, and then stronger arms pulled her to her feet.

"Merry Winger, you're under arrest for three counts of murder," Laura said, as a plane full of passengers looked on, several filming the action with their phones.

Merry glared at her. "Only three?" she asked. "I guess you didn't find the other bombs yet."

"Where are the other bombs?" Jace asked.

"As if I'd tell you." She smiled. "It will be so much better if you find that out for yourself."

Chapter Twenty

"We don't know where Merry Winger planted those last two bombs, but her past behavior should give us some clues." Laura addressed the assembled team, consisting of FBI agents, local police and the county's bomb squad and SWAT. She indicated the list of previous bomb locations. "The first three were detonated at Stroud Pharmaceuticals' administrative offices. The fourth went off at Merry's home, deliberately set there by her to divert suspicion."

"So the most likely location for the fifth and sixth bombs is Stroud Pharmaceuticals," one of the SWAT members said.

"Except Stroud is shut down right now," Ramirez said. "There's no one there to be a target of the bomb."

"Yes, I think the key lies in considering the target," Laura said. "The first two bombs at Stroud killed people other than their intended target. We believe Merry set those bombs intending to kill Donna Stroud, who she saw as standing between her and her goal of marrying Parker Stroud. The third bomb, the one that killed Steve Stroud, may have been intended for Donna also."

"One of the two remaining bombs is probably intended to harm Donna," Jace said. "She's unfinished business for Merry."

"Exactly," Laura said. "We've already contacted Mrs. Stroud and local police have escorted her from her home. We have a team searching there right now."

"What about Parker Stroud?" Rogers studied the white board, arms folded across his muscular chest. "Even though Merry claimed to be in love with him, she threw him under the bus, coming to you with that bank book and her story about seeing him with the castor plant."

Ramirez nodded. "Parker is with his mother at a safe location now, but we should have a team search his house, too."

Laura surveyed the faces of those before her, each tense with the knowledge that lives depended on them making the right guess and finding those bombs. "Any other ideas?"

"We should talk to Leo," Ramirez said. "Maybe Merry told him something about who she intended to target."

Laura mentally kicked herself for not thinking of this earlier. "Great idea," she said. "Let's do it."

Leo was still being held in the local jail, so twenty minutes later Laura, Ramirez, Jace and

Rogers crowded into an interview room where Leo Elgin waited. Dressed in a baggy orange jumpsuit, his hair in need of a trim, he looked younger than his twenty-three years.

"We've arrested Parker Stroud for your mother's murder," Jace said. "He's admitted putting the ricin into the bottles of Stomach Soothers."

Leo stared at him. "Parker?" He wet his lips. "Why would he do something like that?"

"Apparently, he was embezzling money from Stroud Pharmaceuticals," Laura said. "Your mother noticed some discrepancies in the accounts and confronted him. He killed her to keep her from going public with the information. We believe the other deaths were to hide what he'd done and divert suspicion away from him."

Pale and clearly shaken, Leo shook his head. "I thought he was my friend. He was always trying to help me."

"Maybe he felt guilty," Rogers said. He sat in the chair across from Leo. "We've also arrested Merry Winger. She told us you sold her the bombs that killed Lydia Green, Angela Dupree and Steven Stroud."

"I sold her the bombs," he said. "She never told me what she was going to do with them."

"Weren't you a little curious?" Rogers asked.

Leo shook his head, emphatic. "I didn't want to know."

"So some woman comes up to you, says she

wants you to make her six bombs and you're like, 'Sure. No problem'?" Rogers tilted his head to one side and squinted at Leo. "If this is a side business of yours, building bombs to order, who else have you sold explosives to?"

"Nobody else, I swear."

"So Merry was the first person you made bombs for?" Laura stood behind Rogers and addressed Leo.

"Yes."

"You didn't think it was strange she wanted you to make a bomb—much less six of them?" Laura asked.

"She promised to find the person who killed my mother!" He buried his head in his shackled hands and the room fell silent. Laura scarcely breathed.

At last, Leo raised his head and looked at her, his eyes filled with sadness. "Look, I know it was wrong, but I was so angry. My mother was dead and she died a horrible death. I wanted the people responsible to pay, and Merry convinced me she wanted to help."

"But why a bomb?" Rogers asked. "Why not more poison?"

"She said she had heard I was the mad bomber." He flushed. "I tried to tell her that was just a stupid kid stunt, but she went on and on about it. She…she flattered me. She was really pretty and

I was lonely and…" His voice trailed away and he shrugged, his cheeks flushed.

"But how did you know how to build the bombs?" Rogers asked. "Had you done something like this before?"

"No, but I found a lot of information on the internet. And I work with trip alarms all the time, so setting the trigger wasn't all that different."

"What did you think when you heard Lydia Green and Angela Dupree died because of bombs you built?" Ramirez asked.

Leo bowed his head again. "I felt terrible. I panicked and called Merry and tried to get her to return the rest of the bombs. But she wouldn't. She said I didn't need to worry, that everything would work out and the two of us would go away together."

"Where were you going to go?" Laura asked.

"Australia. Or maybe New Zealand." He looked away again. "I guess you think I'm pretty dumb, but she made me believe her."

"There are two more bombs that haven't exploded," Jace slid into the chair next to Leo. "We need to find them before some other innocent person gets hurt. Do you have any idea where Merry put them?"

"No." He angled his body toward Jace. "I promise if I knew I'd tell you. I don't want anyone else to die."

Laura's phone signaled an incoming text. She checked the display.

#5 safely removed from D. Stroud's home. Nothing at P. Stroud's

She glanced up. Jace was checking his phone also. He looked up and held her gaze. *We're getting close*, he seemed to say.

"Leo, did Merry ever mention a name of any particular person she wanted to take out with the bombs?" Laura asked.

"No. We never talked about it. She knew it upset me and she said she would rather talk about me. About us." He had the same dumbfounded look as a kid who had just learned Santa Claus wasn't real. Part of him couldn't believe Merry had lied about wanting to be with him.

"We need to go," Laura said abruptly, and left the room.

Jace hurried after her. "Why the rush?" he asked, catching up to her at the end of the hall. "What set you off?"

"He's still in love with her. She used him to kill three people so far and if she walked in that door right now and said she was ready to run away with him, he'd leave right away, if he could."

"I agree it's twisted, but it's nothing we haven't seen before."

"It just struck me how often love has been used

to manipulate people in this case," she said. "Not just Leo, but Parker, too. Merry professed to love him and want to be his wife, but really all she wanted was his money. And even Donna Stroud refused to let Parker have a bigger say in running the company when he could have been a real help to her. Instead, she tried to cover up the severity of her husband's dementia and run things on her own, probably out of love."

"So love—or the wrong kind of love, or the wrong idea of love, can lead people to do bad things," Jace said. "We know that. But we also know the right kind of love can lead to truly wonderful things." He slid one arm around her waist and pulled her close.

She turned to him, fighting against the anguish building inside her. "What are we going to do after this case is over?" she asked.

To his credit, he didn't flinch, or ask her to explain what she meant. "What do you want to do?" he asked.

"We won't be pretending anymore to be husband and wife," she said. "We won't be living together, but we'll still be working together."

"I was getting used to seeing you when I wake up in the morning and at dinner every night," he said. His voice had the low, seductive quality that usually made her weak at the knees, but right now it just made her want to cry. "I was even getting used to all the vegetables you keep feeding me."

She pulled away from him, needing space to think. "Office romances are a bad idea," she said.

"There's nothing against them in the regulations. The Bureau has a history of accommodating married couples."

"Who said anything about marriage?" Panic clawed at her throat. This was Jace she was talking to. Not Jace Lovejoy, her pretend husband, but wild man Jace, who was reckless and cocky and everything she was not.

"I'm not trying to rush you," he said. "I'm just pointing out that if our supervisors don't have a problem with relationships between agents, why should you?"

"I can't talk about this now."

Something flared in his eyes, and she readied herself for a verbal battle. Maybe that was what she had wanted all along, to pick a fight that would lead to them breaking up. At least then she would prove she couldn't depend on a man like him.

"All right," he said, his voice even. "We won't talk now, but we need to talk later."

She didn't have to come up with an answer to that, because Ramirez and Rogers joined them. "We need to go through the list of Stroud employees," Ramirez said. "We think one of them will be the most likely target of the last bomb. You have a list, don't you?"

"It's on my laptop at the trailer," Laura said. "I'll go get it."

"I'll come with you," Jace said.

"No, you stay here." She looked at the other two. If she glanced at him, she might give away all her mixed-up feelings. "You should talk to Merry. See what she has to say. Jace can help with that."

"All right," Ramirez said. "We were just on our way to interview her."

Laura left before Jace could weigh in with his opinion. All she wanted was a little time alone to pull herself together. She needed to bring her focus back to the case, away from the man who had turned her life upside down.

JACE STARED AFTER LAURA. Just when he thought he had torn down the protective wall she had built around herself, she was working hard to build it back up again.

"Come on," Ramirez said. "Let's see if we can get anything out of Merry."

He had expected Merry to be afraid. She had no criminal record and for most people, being handcuffed, fingerprinted and photographed, and locked in a cell was a terrifying experience.

But Merry held her head up and looked him in the eye when he and Ramirez entered the interview room. "Where's Laura?" she asked.

"She had something else to do," Jace said.

"She didn't want to face me, did she?" Merry said.

"Would you prefer that Laura be here for this interview?" Ramirez asked. "I can get her."

"No way." Merry waved her hand in front of her face as if shooing away a fly. "I never liked her. Why would I want her here now?"

Ana sat across from Merry while Jace stood by the door. "Tell us about the bombs," Ramirez said after she had completed the preliminaries for the recording. "Why did you decide to set them?"

"You can't ignore a bomb, or pretend it was an accident. A little mistake. Bombs make a statement."

"What statement do they make?"

"I'm here and you're not going to ignore me."

"Who was ignoring you?" Ramirez asked.

"The Strouds ignored me. They thought I wasn't good enough for their perfect son." She sniffed. "I wonder if Donna thinks he's so perfect now that she knows he's a murderer."

"We found the fifth bomb, in Donna Stroud's car," Ramirez said. "We safely removed it and Donna is fine."

Merry frowned and said nothing.

"Where is the sixth bomb?" Jace asked.

Merry shifted her gaze to him. "You really haven't figured that out?"

"No," he admitted.

She looked amused. "Don't worry, you will."

The look in her eyes froze Jace. Ramirez asked another question and Merry looked away, but the smugness in Merry's gaze was burned on his retinas. She thought she had gotten away with something.

Revenge on someone she didn't like.

He left the room, pulling out his phone as he walked. He texted Laura. Come back. Don't go into the trailer. DON'T.

He punched in her number and listened to the call going through, running now. Then he remembered Laura had the truck. He grabbed a passing officer. "I need your keys."

The cop stared at him. "My keys?"

Laura wasn't answering her phone. Why wasn't she answering her phone? "Your car keys. I need your car keys." He dug out his badge and flipped it open. "It's an emergency."

Something in Jace's expression persuaded the man. He dug a bunch of keys from his pocket. "It's a blue Nissan Rogue, in the employee lot."

Jace found the car and started it, then fastened his seat belt with one hand while he hit Redial for Laura's number. "Pick up the phone!" he ranted as he peeled rubber on the turn from the parking lot.

He drove like a man possessed, barreling down the road with his emergency flashers on, sounding the horn at anyone who got in his way. Laura's phone went to voice mail. He ended the call and hit Redial again.

He was still half a mile from the trailer when she answered. "Sorry, I was on another call. What do you need?"

"Where are you?" he demanded, the car careening wildly as he took a sharp curve at speed.

"I'm just at the trailer. Give me a second."

"Don't go in." His heart pounded as if it would burst from his chest. He could hardly control the car on the rough road. "The bomb. I think the bomb is in the trailer," he said.

"The bomb?"

But he was already racing up the driveway, the car fishtailing as he braked hard and slid to a stop behind the truck.

Laura stood, halfway up the walk, gaping at him. He burst from the car, ran to her and pulled her close.

"Jace, what is going on?" she asked, her voice muffled against his chest.

"I was almost too late." His voice broke, and he could feel the tears hot on his cheeks, but he didn't care. He looked down at her. "I almost lost you," he said.

"I'm right here." She cupped his face in both hands and kissed him. A tender, comforting kiss that he never wanted to end.

The cop whose car he had borrowed arrived first, with Rogers and Ramirez, followed by a bomb squad with a German shepherd that alerted on the front door. "There's a bomb here, all right," a heavily helmeted man called. "Clear the area."

Laura insisted on driving. Shaken as she was, Jace looked worse. He said nothing as she drove, not to police headquarters, where the others were headed, but to the lake, where they had spied on Leo and Parker. Was that really only ten days ago?

She parked in the lot and turned off the engine. They sat in silence for a long moment, the distant sounds of laughter and muffled conversation drifting to them on a hot breeze through the open windows.

"I guess it's over now," Jace said.

"Everything but the paperwork," Laura said.

"We can go back to Knoxville and our normal lives," he said.

Except her life would never be the same again. She unfastened her seat belt and turned toward him. "What you said before, about us. Being a couple."

"Yes?"

"I want to try. When you came running up to me outside the trailer—no one has ever looked at me that way before—as if I was the most precious thing in the whole world."

"That's because to me, you are."

He pressed the button to release his own seat belt and slid over to her. She tilted her head up for his kiss, but he merely smoothed her hair back from her forehead. "I love you, Laura Smith," he said. "I love how you always play by the rules because you recognize how quickly things can fall apart without them. I love that you're brave but not reckless, and you have the courage to try new things, even when it makes you uncomfortable."

"You make me uncomfortable." She slid her hand around the back of his neck. "In a good way."

"I'll keep working on that." He started to kiss her, but she held him off. "What?" he asked.

"I love you, too. And I've never said that to a man before." She swallowed. "Not even my dad. Do you think that's strange?"

The lines around his eyes tightened. "It's not strange," he said, his voice rough with emotion. "And I'm honored to be the first."

Then he did kiss her, and she fell into the kiss, diving in deep into this crazy lake of emotion that frightened her and thrilled her and made her happier than she had ever thought she could be.

* * * * *